MILES

STEELE RIDERS MC 2ND GENERATION
BOOK 4

C.M. STEELE

The Steele Press

Miles had known Elsa her entire life, watched her grow, protected her, cared for her, but the moment she stumbled into his arms, something shifted. She's no longer the little girl from his memories. She's the woman he wants to spend forever with. All he has to do is wait for the right moment to claim her... but one misstep, and suddenly she's furious, ready to tear him apart.

Elsa has loved Miles for as long as she can remember and denied it just as long. One foolish kiss shattered her carefully built walls, leaving her humiliated and her heart aching. Now, every glance, every touch, every reminder of what she can't have twists the knife deeper. She needs space to heal, to move on... but Miles refuses to let her go.

He insists she needs his protection from the danger lurking in the shadows. However, the only threat Elsa feels is the one he poses to her heart because no matter how much she tries to push him away, she can't stop wanting the man who's determined to make her his.

CHAPTER ONE

MILES

"Thank you for hosting this dinner, Miles. I've always considered you a son, and your father one of my greatest friends." I don't need his appreciation, but I treasure it. This man has always been wonderful to me and is the reason I'm so damn successful. Of course, my own father has a lot to do with that as well. I can't diminish that aspect, but Emiliano Martín was instrumental in the man I've become—especially because I've chosen to live in Vegas instead of Steeleville like my father.

He takes a seat behind his desk, looking worse for wear as a grunt escapes him. He tries to hide it, but it's pointless. The man isn't that young anymore, so I'm not sure why he bothers. Given all he's been through, I know the pain is intense, and there is no shame in dealing with it.

"Are you well?" I ask my godfather, who seems a little under the weather since I saw him two days ago.

1

"Yes," he remarks. "The surgery is in two days, but the damn pain is a son of a bitch now." I nod.

"Do you need me to call the doctor, get you some meds, or call my godmother?" She'd do anything to take care of him.

His eyes widen, and he leans back in his chair. "Oh, God, no. Don't call Roxie." His voice amplified and his shoulders stiffed. Hell, that stressed him more than normal. He loves her, so it's not that he doesn't want her around. Their love was unshakeable, so something has to be up.

I tilt my head and take a seat in the chair in front of his desk. I wonder if there's something I'm missing. "How is my godmother?"

"She is managing, doing her best not to worry, and I don't want to add to her worries. We haven't told the kids about the risks, but they're smart." He calls them kids, but they are pretty much all adults now, so they know that the risks are great but the surgery is necessary. That's why I'm willing to allow all these pieces of shit into my home for a discussion. There's no way in hell I'd allow them in my home otherwise.

The families have to be made aware that Elsa is under my protection. The entire Martín family is under my protection, but that's the most important part of the meeting. She is a prize that men want to claim, and I'm certain that those assholes are going to bring her up.

"Does Elsa know about the dinner?" I ask.

"No, she doesn't, and we need to keep it that way." He's always done a great job of keeping the women out of the dangerous end of our lives. It's for the best given how easily his enemies would love to use them to their advantage.

"Good. I don't want her to get the wrong idea. She's just a little girl—and my godsister." I have no interest in her other than protecting her from the dangers that come with being a beautiful heiress, and she is beautiful—remarkably so. I haven't seen her in the past year, surprisingly, because life has gotten in the way, but as it is, I need to do a better job.

"She's hardly a little girl anymore, but I want her safe."

"Don't worry about her. I won't let anything happen to little Elsa."

"You keep referring to her as little, but she's about to start her second year of college soon."

My eyes widen like a damn clown. I rub my jaw and then add, "Damn—second year? Where have I been?" I've been working nonstop for the company and helping with problems that arise in Steeleville from time to time, so much that I don't have any social life, and it's a shame that I haven't even kept up with those closest to me.

"Working your ass off. I'm sure Milo has mentioned it once or twice."

Hardly. Now that I think about it, he actually makes a concerted effort not to mention Elsa to me. "Not that often.

3

Just that she's a pain in the ass." A thought comes to mind, and I push it back, but it lingers. There is no way that Milo saw the way I looked at her that day. It was brief, and I was just stunned. Elsa had surprised us one day in a tiny pair of shorts and a cartoon tee with her hair in a ponytail. It wasn't anything super attention-grabbing, but I noticed that she'd grown up. I quickly excused myself to attend a meeting, and that was the last time I saw her. Hell, that was over a year ago.

"Ha. Siblings. Go figure. She's a good girl, but headstrong like her mother and extremely anxious to be independent." I know what he means by that: no damn security, free to be like every other girl around her. That isn't something that can easily be done because of who she is.

I walk over to the liquor cabinet and pour myself a drink. "What is she studying? It's not like she wants to take over the hotel." I know that because her brother and I have already split the daily operations and control of the Granite hotels, and now the added casino next door. She has no interest in such things, but she does reap the benefits of its success.

She has four brothers, but only Milo is old enough and wants to be a part of the business. Julio is in college in New York, Miguel is currently in high school, and Daniel is just a kid still.

"You're going to laugh when I tell you." I raise my eyebrow, waiting to learn what ridiculous path she chose. She loves dogs, so maybe she's going to be a vet. That would suit her. "Criminology."

"Are you serious? She picked that. Would you care for one?" I ask, waving my glass.

"No, it's off-limits for me for a bit." Damn. I needed more than a drink when it came to that news.

"Fine, I'll drink for the both of us. She does know that not everything in our world is always aboveboard." We aren't criminals per se, but we aren't squeaky clean either. Okay, we were dirtier than most, but not for the sake of being dirty. We got our hands filthy when necessary.

"Yes, but she's difficult." I need to have a talk with the spoiled little princess. She's already got more than most girls will ever have, and she is on the verge of losing her father, but the little brat wants to learn ways to catch bad guys. Does she suddenly detest her father?

A rapid knock on the door comes, and I go to open it, only to nearly be steamrolled by a five foot three little fireball. I catch her before she falls, but I'm assailed by her scent and the insane pounding in my chest. "Oh my goodness, Miles. I hadn't... I didn't see you there," she stammers.

"What's up, Princess?" her dad answers as she tries to untangle herself from my arms, but I have a strong hold on her. A hold that locks into place as if our lives depended on it.

My mind didn't make up the brief encounter last year. Damn it. Little Elsa has grown into a beautiful woman with captivating caramel, tiger eyes. My heart is racing like it has never done before. She's shockingly more perfect with her stunned expression. Foolishly, I want to drag her lips to mine.

C.M. STEELE

Even with the news that my godfather needs surgery and that life is going to get a little more difficult with the troubles, nothing compares to the way she looks up at me with her lips parted, her hands on my forearms. Even through my suit, I can feel her touch burning me, marking me.

"Excuse me," I cough, releasing her so I can breathe. When was the last time I'd seen her? Was it her eighteenth birthday? God, that was so long ago. She looked breathtaking then, but an emergency came up and I had to leave before even greeting her.

"There's someone here to see you," she says, looking right past me toward her father.

"Okay. Do you know who it is?" I'm surprised she didn't already tell him who it was; unless she didn't want to say it in front of me which is strange.

She smiles and rolls her eyes. "Oh of course, sorry. It's the doctor. Mom told me to come get you."

"I'll accompany you," I offered, needing to get some air and space between me and the sweet temptation that's my little godsister.

"Actually, you could probably discuss Elsa's plans for college. You two haven't seen each other in, what? A year or more?" he suggests, raising his brows. I'm not sure his motives. Can he tell I'm interested and he's trying to torture me before he actually tortures me, or does he want me to talk her out of criminology?

6

"I don't think he cares. He has better things to do with his time," she mutters, clearly offended, and I can't blame her but it was for her own good. He gives me a warning glance to make this right before walking out the office door, closing it behind him.

That might not have been the wisest thing to do. The temperature doubled in the room instantly. "That's not fair, little princess. I apologize for neglecting you, but I have time, and I am quite intrigued about your major."

"Are you really?" She raises her head, and for a moment I see the hesitation before she turns a snarky smile on me. Fuck, there's the reaction I knew my body would have if we spend time together.

"Yes. Tell me all about it." I lean on the edge of her father's desk with my feet out in a relaxed pose, arms crossed.

"I'm planning on studying criminal justice with a focus on forensics." I raised one eyebrow.

"Interesting. A particular type of forensics?" I ask. I'm sure she's taking her gen-eds now.

"Particular types?" she asks, tilting her head as if she isn't already a year in.

"Yes—digital, anthropology, fingerprinting, toxicology, etc."

She smiles as she slaps her forehead. "Oh, duh. I want to learn about physical forensics, so more toward anthropology." Fuck, she's adorable when she's flustered.

"Are you nervous, Princess?"

"No," she sputters out defensively, turning red. I hide a chuckle and straighten myself up to hide the uncomfortable arousal in my pants that is no longer easily disguised.

"Well, maybe we can discuss things when you get a little further along in your classes since I have a degree in computer forensics. We can compare notes on techniques and cases."

"I've taken an anthropology course and it was fun, but it was just an intro class." She tries to minimize her experience because she thinks I won't find it interesting, but I've suddenly found myself interest in all things Elsa.

"That's great. Did you get to handle any artifacts?" I like the way her face lights up.

"Yes. It was pretty cool and even a skull from a neolithic hunter-gather. It's so different than ours. The brow ridge is much more defined." Why the fuck am I jealous of her touching another man's face?

"Do you usually going around staring at men's brow ridges?"

"No, but it's going to be a part of forensics and human anatomy. Do you actually work cases?"

"Yes, but I can't discuss things like that." I wink at her, and the apples of her cheeks turn an adorable pink. I've lent my expertise in things, both legally and underhandedly. Most people would be surprised how often the government works with the dark side of life.

"Fine. I suppose we'll see about it one day." She relaxes, and her body becomes light and bubbly as she speaks. I need to walk away before I get too comfortable around her. There is too much going on to figure out this attraction I'm feeling.

"Good. If you need anything, give me a call. Do you have my number?" I ask, wanting a reason for her to call me. Damn, I want her to come with me and present her tonight at my side. No one would dare question her place or consider her an option. That's not possible for many reasons. I'm nearly five years older than her, her father would kill me for just claiming his daughter without his approval, and the most important one, she has to want me too.

"No, I don't think I do." She shakes her head as her pretty eyes squint. It almost feels like an insult because her number is in mine under "Princess." I pull out my phone and search for her name, then hit dial. It rings in her pocket.

"You have my number?" The shock on her face is so adorable that I want to close the distance and touch her, but I can't.

"Yes. Of course I do. I've had it since you got it. I have all those that are close to my godfather," I inform her.

"Oh, that makes sense." Her face shifts, and then she drops her head to focus on her phone, saving my number. Once she's done, she looks up with a smile and asks, "How is your family?"

"They're great. My parents should be visiting soon and I'm sure they'll want to have a big family get together."

"That would be wonderful." She rocks back and forth on her heels, biting down on her bottom lip, trying to look anywhere around the room where I don't take up space. If I wanted, I could close the distance and force her to stare at me, but I let her off easy.

She has no idea what I'd do if I caved and decided that she was mine. I learned a long time ago that I'm a man who likes power and control. Anyone who dares to take what belongs to me would lose. Anyone who comes between us would perish. I feel my body tighten as the tension builds. I need to make my excuses and get out of here. Sliding my hand in my pocket, I pull out my phone, checking it.

"Sorry, Elsa, but I just got a text. I'm needed at the casino." As much as I'd love to linger in her presence, it's a foolish mistake.

Her body language immediately shifts to a cold, closed-off expression. "Oh, it's okay. I hope everything is all right."

"I'm sure it is, but you know they need the boss's approval." I wink and walk around her to the doorway, hoping that she sees I don't dislike her. "Take it easy, and don't talk to strangers, especially boys. College guys may be charming, but they have nothing to offer at their age." My voice is cold and controlling, but I'm deadly serious. My men will be added to her security to ensure to her safety and little frat fucks stay away from my future wife.

"Thanks, Miles. Don't want to keep your people waiting." I know I fucked up and offended her, but I have to let it go and walk out of the room without closing the door behind me.

My movements are rapid and necessary. When I enter the foyer, the doctor is departing as well. "I didn't know she could scare you off," her father chuckled.

"No, I have a matter to handle at the casino." It doesn't matter that I continue the lie.

"Do I need to be concerned?"

"Not at all. Just the usual issues." He nods and I shake his hand and finally greet the doctor with a light jut of my chin.

"Oh, Mr. Ivanov, it's quite good to see you. You're looking in peak health." My godfather gives him a curious look as he walked him toward the door.

"Yes, I should hope so. I'm a bit young to be taking a nosedive." I arch my eyebrow. I'm glad my godfather's surgical team was recommended by those in Steeleville and not here. I don't quite trust their motives.

"Don't misunderstand, Mr. Ivanov. I meant only that you seem extra spirited at the moment. Perhaps I misspoke."

"Oh, Daddy, I didn't know you still had company." The doctor gives me a slight glance, and I glare at him to mind his next words.

"Actually, we were all just leaving," I add.

"It was good to see you both. I hope the dinner tonight is successful. Keep me informed." My godfather's words are measured, but I understand.

"I will," I remark. As both the doctor and I step outside, he smirks and says, "Oh, to be young again. Good luck, and if you are lucky enough to land such a young lady, don't mess it up; some of us don't get to start again."

"She's too young and under my protection," I inform him and enter my vehicle, effectively closing the discussion that is none of his business. "Soon, Elsa, soon," I mutter to myself as I drive off.

FOUR MEN GATHER AROUND MY DINING TABLE, EACH OF THEM with their guards in the other room, unable to be far away. The food has been set up around the table, wine poured, and then I stand up and address the group. "Gentlemen, I've invited you here tonight to discuss some matters."

The arrogant Antonio Santos puts his palm out and interrupts my next words. "We know why you invited us here."

"Did I ask you to fucking speak?" I state as I stare him down, daring him to challenge me. Each of these men are the same age of my godfather and I'm the same as their sons who are a bunch of pussies. I could mop the floor with each of their boys, both physically and mentally. My wealth and success have been earned, so these bastards will give me my due respect or they will suffer.

"Look, kid, we're not here to negotiate anything. We understand Martín's in a predicament, and if he's not careful, his empire could crumble." They are playing a dangerous game.

"Watch your fucking mouth or you'll lose your tongue. I might be young, but I'm not someone to play with. I expect civility and respect in my home. I offered you a lovely meal, great wine, and excellent hospitality. Now I ask you to show me some respect, or else." His jaw tics, but he then backs down and sits properly, simmering down before I show him why I'm in charge.

"He's right, Santos. The young man has great skills and has shown us why he follows in Martín's footsteps," Novak interjects.

"You're not even his son," Rotello adds. "Why isn't he speaking on his own behalf?"

I scoff. "No, I'm his godson, and I've been a part of his family for a long time. He is currently handling matters for the family hotels."

"Speaking of family, that daughter of his is just the right age for a family; many of us have sons."

I try to keep my composure, but the mere mention of her sets my teeth on edge, and I can't hold back. "There will be no talk of Elsa; she is not for anyone else."

"Oh, is that how it is?" Rotello says. The room erupts with murmurs, ridiculous smirks, and condescending grins.

"So you want to be his son in more ways than one?" Santos adds, smirking like he's got some inside knowledge.

I slam my hand on the table, drawing their full attention back to me. "Gentlemen, Elsa's free to make her own choice when she's ready; however, it will be none of your sons. Am I clear on that? She's under my protection, just like the rest of the Martín house, and that includes keeping her away from all the families."

I get a couple more smirks and grimaces, but the matter is dropped. "Now let's enjoy this wonderful meal before it goes cold."

"I can second that," Novak says, swirling his spoon in the soup. Everyone begins to eat, and the tension slowly dies down. The rest of the evening carries on with some heated business discussion and shady political dealings. Two hours later, the night comes to an end. I can't wait to get those sons of bitches out of my home. I have my home secured and searched for any mysterious cameras or listening devices once they depart.

Hopefully they heed my warnings, and my godfather pulls through. I'm not sure how we got so mixed up with the families in the first place. We aren't technically criminals, but the elements are always around us, intruding on our existence, making every legal avenue difficult to navigate. Sometimes our hands get dirty, but this warning will be my most serious because I'm willing to do anything to protect the family, especially Elsa.

I ENTER THE WAITING ROOM WHERE ELSA SITS IN A CHAIR BY herself. Her eyes dart upward, spotting me, and my heart nearly cracks in half as I see the tears in her eyes. I haven't received any negative news, but I know it's not because something bad has happened. She's worried and scared because it's her daddy. My heart hurts for her—she needs comfort. Also, I got here as soon as I could. Before I can react, she's out of her seat.

"I'm so worried about him, Miles," Elsa sobs, wrapping her arms around my waist and pressing her face into my chest. Fuck, it takes all of my willpower not to cave to the growing desire, but we are in the hospital for her father. Still, I allow the indulgence of my hands on her waist.

"He's going to be fine. You know your father. He's insanely strong and stubborn." I chuckle, attempting to lighten the severe mood.

"You probably think because I'm young that I'm being foolish and overreacting," she huffs, looking up at me with her tear-stained face, gently pushing away from me. I don't fully let her go.

"You're not overreacting, Princess. I don't like seeing those tears on your beautiful face." I cup her flushed cheek and swipe my thumb across it, wiping away a lone tear. "You shouldn't ever have to hurt, Elsa."

Before I realize what is happening, her lips are pressed against mine. I freeze, mouth closed, unable to process the softness of her sweet mouth on my lips. It's like my brain short fucking circuits. The sound of footsteps prevents me from responding, and she wrests herself away. She pulls back before I can respond.

"Hey, Elsa, are you okay?" her brother asks. He raises his brow at me and then looks at her with brotherly concern.

"Um, yeah. I'm going to check on Mom." She wipes her eyes and then walks away without looking at either of us.

After she leaves, her brother, one of my closest friends, sighs. "I'm sorry, bro. I saw that."

I groan, stuffing my hands in my pockets, trying to cover the uncomfortable fact that I'm half-staffed right now.

"I'm sure she's just upset and confused with a huge schoolgirl crush on you."

"Yeah, and I think I just made it worse. She's vulnerable and needs comfort."

"Don't worry. I'll take care of her. Just make sure that the rest of the families stay away from her. The way she's feeling right now, she might be putty in any of these slick fuckers' hands." As soon as he says that, the words infuriate me.

I leave the hospital on a mission to re-establish my role as the protector of this family and of Elsa. By the end of the night, every family is aware that I will be handling all business meetings, and no one is allowed to even speak with Elsa unless we allow it. As soon as my godfather is all cleared and the families around us aren't trying to come after us, I'm taking the time to claim Elsa.

"He's not out of the woods yet, but the surgery went well and he's awake," Milo says as I take his call in my library.

"Good. Tell him I expect him back at work soon," I tease. Although knowing him, I'm sure he'll try.

"He said you'd say that," he says with a chuckle.

"How is Elsa?"

"She's fine now that my dad is better. She said that kiss was just a thank you because she was upset."

"Well, I hope she isn't going around thanking other fuckers like that."

"We know she's not, but she won't admit to it. She said she did have a crush, but that stopped when she was seventeen and started dating Jacob. He took her to prom."

"Of course not. Well, I'm going to get some sleep because while some people are just lying about being lazy, some of us have to work." I'm going to look up this fuck named Jacob. He's a dead man.

"I'll tell him you said that." I laugh and hang up. I'm sure my godfather will be up and working before the doctor clears it, but my godmother won't allow that shit. I'm grateful that he's going to make it, but it seems someone else won't.

CHAPTER TWO

ELSA

Summer seems to drag by with visits from Miles becoming more and more frequent to check in on my father. It irks me as much as it excites me. Not once do we speak about the forbidden, hideous mistake of a kiss, if I can call it that. My first kiss was a sham. I planted my lips on the man I've been crushing on since I can remember, only for him to go stone cold in the middle of the hospital waiting room and my brother to walk in and save him from me.

God, I don't know what's worse: the mortifying look on Miles's face, or the conversation with my brother afterwards.

He pulled me aside and asked, "Have you lost your damn mind? Miles is my friend and a huge part of the family. He isn't the kind of man to love anybody. It would be foolish for you to fall in love with a man who would only hurt you in the end because it would cause a war between us."

"Why would you say something like that?" I asked him.

"Miles doesn't date people. He's all about business and power; you don't fit anywhere in there. The man is stone cold, and I mean that in the best of ways in other things, but when it comes to love? Well, I don't want to see you hurt."

"Thanks, but it was spur of the moment."

"I hope you don't go around thinking of people like that."

"Of course not. I was extremely emotional, and it wouldn't happen again anyway. Now, will you leave me alone so I can go into a hole and disappear?"

"Relax. It's no big deal."

"You're over here scolding me, so I think it's a big deal."

"Trust me, Miles will forget about it. He's got more important things to worry about."

"I got it. I know I'm on the bottom of Miles's totem pole list."

"Good. I don't want to see you hurt."

"Thank you. I love you, bro." He gives me a giant brotherly squeeze.

"I love you, too. You deserve someone special who's going to treat you great."

"You don't think highly of Miles, do you?"

"I do. It's just that he's not a man who wants a wife. I've never *heard him mention it once. If he did, I think he'd make a great husband, but until that day comes..."*

I can't believe how naively stupid I was. Maybe he's aware of how mortified I was and is taking pity on me, or he's doing his best to avoid the situation as well. Maybe my brother's right, and he's just forgotten the incident entirely. Either way, it's for the best.

Unfortunately, we're all going to Steeleville together. We're going to be locked in on one massive private jet to visit his family and ours for the annual gathering of all the Steele Riders. Last year he wasn't even there, so everyone is going to be excited to see him. I have to stop myself from rolling my eyes.

All the non-related, unmarried girls will be gushing over him, while I do my best to pretend I hate him. I'm returning to college next week, and then I'll be seeing a lot less of Mr. Miles "High and Mighty" Ivanov. Goodness —*Miles Ivanov.* What kind of name is that anyway? Seriously, what were his parents thinking? As if making his first name gentle was going to help him be less dark and dangerous. The bastard has to be twice as attractive as he is mysterious.

"Are we ready?" my father asks, passing by my open bedroom door.

"Yes, I am." I start rolling my suitcase to the door, and then Miles pops up. "What the hell?" I squeak.

"Young lady," Miles gasps, pressing his hand to his mouth. The humor in his eyes makes me want to kick him in his shins, but my parents would scold me and it's only another win for him.

"Whatever. You scared me. Why are you stalking me?"

"I'm not stalking, Princess. I offered to carry your suitcase so your father doesn't have to do it."

"I can do it myself, you know." The rush of anger shoots through my body as well as the desire for this man. Why does he have to torment me like this? Always around, always helping while I'm suffering from my crushed heart.

"Your father doesn't want you to do it, and was about to take it, damn it. Don't give me an attitude. Just say 'okay' and 'thank you, Miles.'"

"Thank you, Miles," I sneer.

"Good girl. Was that so hard?" he asks, lightly taking a peek over my head into my messy bedroom.

"Yes, terribly so," I huff, closing my bedroom door quickly so he can't see the chaos. I didn't mean to leave it that way, but I couldn't figure out what to wear and now it's like my damn closet exploded.

"Your future husband is definitely going to need to hire a maid."

"I'd love to see what your bedroom looks like," I bite out.

"What was that, Elsa?" my mother gasps behind us.

"Mom, it's not like that." I can feel the heat flood my face.

"I'll take that for you now." He takes my suitcase and then

my mother's and walks away after causing another damn blunder to come tumbling from my mouth.

"Damn it, I really do hate that man."

"The lady doth protest too much," my mother utters just above a whisper as she passes by with a light laugh. She has no idea about the kiss and how, even now, he continues to make me feel so confused.

"Ugh, whatever. He better not damage my brand-new suitcase or he's buying me a new one."

"Who do you think bought you those?"

"Ugh, why?"

"Ladies, we need to get a move on," my dad hollers from the bottom of the stairs.

"Come on, or we're going to be late." I'm not sure why it matters since it's our plane, but I'm not going to argue because I'm positive Miles is the reason we're being rushed. He probably wants to see his family before the party. We're landing a day early so we have time to relax.

Miles holds the door open for me, as if we don't have a driver there. "Get in, Princess."

"Whatever you say, Mr. Ivanov. I don't want to make us late for our own plane," I scoff, brushing past him and into the vehicle, trying to ignore the way my body vibrates.

"There is a storm coming," my father says.

"Oh," I mutter. Miles smirks as he slides in across from me. I'm not sure if I want to throat punch or kiss the smug bastard. Instead, I do neither. Pulling out my phone, I check my emails for the upcoming school year. There is so much happening next week that I have a lot of planning to do that has nothing to do with Mr. Arrogant. A text comes in from my bestie, and I smile.

ANGE

Can't wait for the fun to begin.

Counting down the minutes

, I text back. The minutes are going to feel like forever being in a confined space with this man.

Maybe you can hang out at my dorm sometimes. I'm living at home, unfortunately, but what can I say—it's pointless to argue with my parents when my safety is a huge concern.

Maybe. We'll see. I might be nineteen, but that doesn't mean I get all the space I want. Being extremely wealthy in Vegas makes me a huge target.

Let me know when you get back.

Okay.

"Ouch," I yelp, lifting my head to glare at Miles.

"Sorry." He bangs my ankle with his big old heavy computer bag. I stare at his monogrammed leather bag, and I want to roll my eyes. I wonder if he has matching cufflinks.

"Dang, what do you have in there?" I grumble, rubbing my ankle.

"Work. Sorry, but I have some matters to handle." He effectively dismisses me and continues to open the bag that is now on his lap.

"Whatever," I mumble under my breath, going back to my phone. It's a damn short ride to the airport, so I don't know why he's bothering with taking anything out.

When our vehicle turns down the road heading toward the casino, my expression twists in confusion. "We have to make two pit stops—one at the hotel, and the other at the casino." That explains why he has time to work and the urgency.

The trip to the casino is fast, but then we stop at the hotel and Miles meets with two women outside the hotel. Both are gorgeous women, and the one in red laced heels obviously can't help but touch his arm twice. I can feel my body shift with tension as they speak. It feels like an eternity.

When he finally returns to the limo, I have to hold my tongue because I'm not anything but the bratty godsister, and I have no right to be jealous even though my entire soul is burning.

"Did she think flirting with you would get a better deal on the booking?" my father asks, seeing the same thing I did.

"I don't know, but I warned her that one more touch and I'd cancel the wedding reception," he states.

"Wedding? You're getting married?" I question, nearly dropping my phone.

"Not anytime soon," my dad answers.

Miles looks at him strangely and then speaks. "The hotel hosts wedding receptions, and the client wants hers there. Although, if that's the way she behaves, I'm not sure she'll make it to the altar."

Unable to come up with a witty response, I nod and sit back with my eyes closed, waiting for the driver to just get us to the airport. It feels like an eternity before we finally arrive and board the plane. Once we are seated, I take a spot far away from him and lay my head back.

"Are you excited to see your cousins?"

"Yes," I answer my mom. "We have some plans to hang out today and visit a couple of shops before the barbecue tomorrow."

"Good. Just stay together and safe."

I roll my eyes. "It's Steeleville. The place is like a fortress."

"Yes, but you know how they are."

"Exactly, and that's why I'm sure we'll be more than safe. Half the town are Riders, and the other half know to keep their hands off of us." It's been easy to stay single even though I'm nineteen when there are beastly guards lurking. Uncle Blade is just as bad as my dad. My only boyfriend, if you could call him that, was Jacob. He asked me out two weeks before prom. We went out like five times, but it was always supervised by my father's loyal spies, and nothing happened.

Jacob took me to prom, and everything was going great until the middle of the night. I started to feel lightheaded. He pulled me off to a corner of the room and became a little too physical. I told him I needed to use the bathroom. Snagging my drink and purse, I used my special test strips, and I realized he drugged it. So, I texted my mother, and before I knew it, I was whisked away moments later and taken home. I didn't see Jacob again.

"Don't take that for granted, Elsa. There are creeps who always have something to prove."

"I won't. It's not like I'm careless."

"I know." She smiles and takes my hand, giving it a squeeze. "You're always so considerate and wise. It's like I've been raising an adult since you were ten, but that doesn't mean I don't worry. The boys are just like your father, which is another kind of headache." She rolls her eyes. My oldest brother runs the hotel with Miles, but he isn't coming this weekend because he has a meeting in Europe.

When we land, my uncle picks us up and Cyber picks up Miles. Finally, we have a break from Miles and I can breathe. I spend the day with my family, and it's so much fun. Tomorrow before the barbecue we are going out shopping all day.

WE BOUGHT TOO MUCH AND OUR BAGS ARE HEAVY, SO WE load them into the trunk of Missy's hybrid. "Girl, I am having way too much fun, but we should get back because I know they're going to be looking for us."

"Relax. My daddy knows where I'm at, and I'm sure your dad knows where you are. Besides, the party doesn't start for an hour, and we don't want to be the first ones there."

"Of course he does, but still."

"Does it have to do with your hot godbrother because, I mean, that guy is intense?"

"It has nothing to do with him," I insist, lying to myself.

"Girl, you're lying," Missy says.

"We know you've had a crush on him for like forever," her younger sister Erica says.

"Come on, we all know that."

"Just because I had a crush on him before doesn't mean anything. I'm so ready to be over everything. I've got to move on from these feelings because I know he doesn't feel the same way."

"Are you serious? Are you sure? Because I totally get a different vibe. When he's around you, it's like he's totally digging you."

I shake my head. "No, he's my father's guard dog. I learned that he's just looking out for me. My father asked him to make sure that we're safe, so don't take my protection as anything more than just that."

"Your father told you that?"

"No, my brother did after an embarrassing moment between Miles and I. Trust me—I'm sure he doesn't want me."

"Damn, that sucks. I'm sorry, girl. Well, we have a lot of hot guys that are Riders now, so we can just introduce you to the rest of them, or maybe you'll meet some of the other guys in town while you're here," Missy offers. I nod.

Erica grips my forearm and squeezes. "Yeah, there's going to be a lot of hot guys at the party, and you can forget all about that jackass."

I smile and cave. "I'm going to try."

"That's the spirit. Let's head back now." We hop into her car and pick up some Starbucks on the way back.

"Ooh, girl, this is just what I needed."

We get back to the party, and involuntarily my eyes look out for Miles even though I'm supposed to meet other men. My gut tells me that it's wrong to want anyone else; still, I can't help how I feel.

We move through the crowd, being greeted by everyone. After about thirty minutes, Missy whispers, "He's not here." He should have been here with his family, but the man does whatever he wants.

I don't know why I expected him to be here. Maybe he's found somebody else to see. After all, he's a hot commodity. I'm sure there's plenty of women in town that would love to hook up with him. Perhaps that's why he pushed me away.

"All right, ladies, show me these guys." My cousin and her bestie walk me around introducing me to several men that I've already met over the years but really don't remember.

"Hey, do you remember Connor?" I wave to him, but he pulls me into a one-armed hug, giving me a good squeeze. How could I forget one of the Steele boys? He's Jackson's son, and Will's cousin. They are like Rider royalty around here.

"Hi, Connor," I answer with a grunt as I feel my air giving out.

He pulls away from me with a wide grin. "God, you're gorgeous."

"Thank you." I'm not good at flirting, so I stand there as if I don't know him, which I really don't. I only come to town like twice a year, and sometimes I don't see everyone.

"So, I hear you're going to UNLV."

I smile and nod. Goodness, every single one of these guys are good looking. "Yeah, that's right."

"Smart and beautiful. It's not going to be long before you're snapped up. I might have to go visit Vegas."

"Maybe you should," my cousin says.

"Where is she?" That deep voice echoes from the distance. I know who it is, but can he be looking for me or someone else? Probably someone else, so I smile at Connor and instantly regret it.

CHAPTER THREE

MILES

I'M SEETHING AS I STALK TOWARD THE SMALL GROUP. THE group that contains one too many unrelated males. The fact that my girl is talking to a single, available man who is eyeing her like candy is pissing me off. He's a family friend, but that can end right now. Jackson reaches them just as I do. Before I can punch Connor in the face, he says, "Son, let me go over something with you really quickly."

"Okay, Pops," he replies with a bit too much mirth. That handsome face needs to be arranged. "Sorry, ladies, catch up with you later." He winks at me with a smugness that's deliberate. "Nice to see you, Miles."

"Whatever. We'll catch up later," I reply, my tone even and flat. We're going to have a nice chat about touching what's not his.

The second he's away from us, my eyes return to the woman who has lit a fire in me that only power and success have before. "And you're in trouble, Princess."

"For what?" her nosy cousin shouts in her defense. Sometimes there are just too many people around us.

"I wasn't talking to you, Erica."

"Rude much?" she adds, annoying me even further.

"Says the person I wasn't speaking to." I readdress my obsession. "You ditched your bodyguards."

She crosses her arms over her ample, yet properly covered chest. Goodness, I'm grateful that she decided not to test my sanity with her outfit today. "I did nothing wrong."

"You weren't in Steeleville—you were in Dallas." It's not where she was, it's her lack of concern for her own safety. She doesn't comprehend the depths to which someone would go to cause her father and myself a lot of pain. Of course, she has no idea that it would obliterate me if something happened to her.

"So. Damn. What. I'm a grown-up." Each word is punctuated through clenched teeth. "Besides, I told my mom that I was going shopping."

"You're still supposed to have security with you."

Elsa tenses for a moment, understanding my concern until her loudmouth cousin speaks up. "Gosh, Miles, lighten up. Old and grumpy already."

"You need to stay out of this; you're already causing

trouble," I warn her accomplice. Their mouths fall open with shock.

"You're rude," my adorable princess reminds me, but it doesn't matter how fucking rude I am because she could have been snagged up in a heartbeat by our enemies, and she has no idea how tempting of a target she is. I'd shown my cards at that dinner. They'd seen the hints of my obsession that has only grown since then.

"You know you're supposed to be protected."

"Well, maybe your guys should have done a better job." She crosses her arms over her waist, lifting her chest. I kept my eyes trained on her face, but I wondered how many other men at the party noticed.

"Yeah, if you want her watched like a damn hawk, then maybe you should do it instead of chasing tail all day, okay?" her cousin continues. Chasing my own tail is more like it. There were matters I had to attend to that required my attention. I would have gladly followed her around, but Simon's attack last winter left me with some business to handle earlier. Luckily, it's all taken care of now.

"Now if you'll excuse us, we have other people to talk to. Come on, Elsa." Her cousin Erica grips her wrist and starts to walk, but then Elsa stops and smiles up at me.

"We're safe here, Miles, so why don't you go and be grumpy somewhere else. You're killing the party," Elsa says, patting my shoulder before walking past me. I want to flip her over my shoulder and out of this place and take her somewhere to spank her little ass.

They begin to move away, and I'm about to grab Elsa's hand to stop her when my father calls out, "A word, Miles."

"Yeah, Dad."

"Let's have a talk." We walk side by side into the clubhouse's security center where we can chat privately. He locks the door and then says, "Have a seat." I don't want to sit, but I also don't defy my father.

I rest my ankle over my knee, attempting to appear relaxed. "What's up, Dad?"

"Are you in love with her?" he asks.

"What do you mean?"

"Son, I'm not fucking blind. I know you take your word seriously and your duty seriously, but most of us have been in your situation before, and we know that look. You're ready to rip Connor's head off, and you know we can't have that." I understand the warning to back off Jackson's boy.

I dip my head and lightly shake it. "Yes... Yes, I'm in love with her." I run my hands through my hair. "At first, I wasn't sure if that's what it was or simply pure arousal... No, who am I kidding? I knew within hours, but it wasn't the right time, and it still isn't. She's young and vulnerable."

"So how long has this been going on?"

"Not that long at all. Right before his surgery. Still, I'm not even sure she really even likes me. Right now, she hates me." I don't even bother mentioning my lustful attraction a year earlier because that shit was inappropriate, and didn't help my cause.

"I don't think so, but if I were you, I'd tread lightly."

"As much as I'd like to make things happen between us, I'm not sure she's ready for what I want. She's busy with school. Besides, there's a little unrest."

My father's shoulders stiffen. "Do you need my help?"

"No. I just got to keep these sons of bitches away from her. I want to give in and make her mine, but I'm not sure if I should risk the distraction."

He laughs. "Son, it's too late. You are hooked and already distracted. Don't worry about the guys here; they all got their warning already. Everyone saw. The warning has already been spread. Not a soul in this place will even try. You looked like a madman."

"Was it *that* bad?"

"Yeah."

"Damn. I've got to work on my obsession, and work on her."

"Nah, you're commanding, Son. Let everyone know where you stand. Just make sure she doesn't get the dark side of you. Save that for the assholes and give your woman the best parts." That I certainly can handle.

"Thanks."

"By the way, I think you need to have a talk with Emiliano." I close my eyes because that's another tough one.

"Yes. We haven't had an official conversation yet. I'm sure he's got questions."

"He does." He winks. "Let's grab a beer and just enjoy some time with family and friends before he grills you about his little girl." I'd prefer to get it over with, but I'd hate to ruin the party if we couldn't agree on my future pursuit of Elsa.

"Sounds good." We walk out and celebrate with everyone. Despite the earlier dramatic nonsense, the party is great. Even Connor doesn't get on my fucking nerves. I do my best to ignore Elsa, letting the team and her family watch her because I don't want to start something I'm not ready to finish.

As the party winds down, I take my leave, saying goodbye to my godparents and letting them know that I'll be taking a different flight back to Vegas in the morning because I have meetings.

"Always working," my godmother says after she pulls me in for a hug.

"It's the way it is," I say, placing a kiss on her cheek. "Today was nice, though." I give a smirk toward Elsa.

"Yes, because every available female couldn't take their eyes off you. You look like you came off a photoshoot instead of a barbecue." Elsa waves her hand up and down toward my body.

"I didn't realize there was a specific attire requirement. I'm pretty sure there are several people here dressed the same way," I remind her as I walk away. Not all of us wore jeans and tee shirts with boots and leather cuts. There's nothing wrong with it. My father has his patch on, and my mother has a cute version that matches her dress, but some of us are wearing slacks, khakis with polos. I like my hair slicked back with neatly trimmed sides. I always keep myself professional, and I don't care what others think except for Elsa. So, I'm going to try to let her comments slide off me as just her residual anger.

As I reach the exit, I'm stopped by my father and hers to say goodbye. "Cyber, your son is something else." Emiliano claps his hand on my shoulder. "He's done wonders to keep my family safe after my surgery, especially my little girl." The tone in his voice is obvious, almost mocking in its intent.

"Yes, we all know how it goes. How emotions suddenly switch on," my father replies, sticking by my side even though I had every intention of handling the situation myself.

"Is that the case, Miles, or am I misjudging?" His brows rise with suspicion.

"Shall we go talk privately?" I ask. They nod, and we walk off to the side of the parked SUVs and climb inside my father's SUV, which is extremely protected and soundproof.

"Like I just explained to my father, my feelings are new, but are firm. Unwavering. I want to marry Elsa one day, and I'm not going to let someone else take her away from me." I make a point of adding that last bit. I might love my godfather, but Elsa has become my number one priority. My loyalty now lies with her even if she doesn't know it yet.

A quiet tension builds in the vehicle. "So, the dinner served a selfish purpose." The accusation hits like hard slap in the face; however, I understood how easily that could be misconstrued.

My words need to be chosen wisely, so I swallow and then take a calming breath. "At first, no, but then she burst through your office door, and it was like I saw a whole new person. I won't deny that I noticed she had changed, but I hadn't realized my feelings until that moment. Elsa was suddenly becoming a woman had to get to know."

"Have you gotten to know her?" he growls. Fuck. Clearly, I chose my words poorly.

"God, no. Not like you're thinking. We barely speak without her wanting to stab me. I'd like to fix our relationship, but I wasn't sure what to do next. The tension is high in Vegas right now, and you were in the middle of recovering. I didn't want to add to the stress. Besides, she has dreams that she's trying to make come true that are more important than my own desires."

"Damn, you have learned a great deal from us."

I smirk. "I have tried."

"Still, your wants should be pretty close to hers," my father adds.

"I hope one day they are, but we both need time. I have too much going on for me to dedicate all my time to her, so I might as well let her focus on school before convincing her to marry me and have a family."

"You don't want her to work?" my godfather asks.

"You don't want her to work, either," I remind him.

"No, I don't, but if she does find a career, I wouldn't stop her."

"It's the same for me, but that's why I'm giving her time. I want her to be happy. She can do that as long as those assholes stay away from her."

"Good boy. That's what I wanted to hear. Now let's get back before our wives start searching for us."

We open the doors, and my mother and godmother are waiting outside, shaking their heads and smiling. "We hope you boys are behaving."

"Always, my love," my father answers with a mischievous grin.

Now to work on my plan to put the Vegas families in order and win Elsa's love. I'm not sure which will be harder.

CHAPTER FOUR

ELSA

"Hey, honey, are you ready to start your first day back?" It's six a.m. and I'm about to head out of the house. I start class at seven. I have four classes this semester for a total of seventeen hours.

"Yes and no. It's going to be a bunch of introductions. Most of the learning starts in the next class."

"How many classes do you have a week?" my father asks, walking into the kitchen in his gym clothes and covered in sweat, clearly done working out for the day. He's looking a lot better, and his movements are sturdier. The hip and knee replacements have gone smoothly.

"I was lucky enough to schedule all my classes on Mondays through Wednesdays, but until six. Tuesday is an online class," I say, smiling and then frowning because it's going to be an insanely long day.

"Are you sure that's a good idea? You're going to be so exhausted."

"Sure, but it's not like I'm in class the whole time. I have two breaks. And look who is talking about being exhausted." I check the time on my phone. "It's just after six, and you're covered in sweat. How many miles did you run?"

"I only did two miles and my strength training. I have to keep in shape for my body to recover. Trust me when I say it's for the best."

"Still, Dad, I want you to be around forever."

"I know, sweetheart," he says, dragging me to his side and pulling me in for a hug. I tug myself away. "Eww, gross. I'm glad I didn't change yet." I roll my eyes and grab my protein shake.

"By the way, I know you hate all the security, so I told them to back off today."

"Thanks, Dad. I appreciate it. They make it hard to get boys to even talk to me."

"I'm not saying they won't be around, but at a very far distance."

"I understand." They walk ten feet behind me most days, which is so damn annoying, so this is a good thing. "I'll take what I can get."

I wave them off and get ready so I can make the short trip to campus. I head to my first class, which thankfully is mercifully short. Math, not my favorite, but a necessary requirement for my degree. Seriously, it's almost enough for me to give up. My teacher is brilliant, but I can't make out what he's saying. I'm going to have to record the lectures and listen to them repeatedly and slowly. His accent is thick and strong. Several classmates near me have their eyes wide open, leaning in as if that's going to help them.

"Hey, don't worry. The notes are on the class page," the guy next to me says.

"Thanks."

"No problem." He winks and then adds, "I'm the TA. He's a great professor, and you'll learn a lot."

"I would if I could get past the heavy accent."

"Yeah, it's a little thick, but it's better if you sit closer to the front."

"I suppose I'll try that next time."

"Or I can tutor you," he offers with a crooked grin. My face flattens, and then I frown.

"Thanks, but no thanks. I will just focus and try to study his inflections," I sneer.

"Oh goodness, please don't take me wrong. I tutor an entire group every semester. It's not one on one. I'm sorry if it came off that way. It's every Wednesday night."

"Oh. My fault," I say begrudgingly. He might actually hold a tutoring session, but I'm wise enough to know that he's full of shit.

"You're still welcome if you feel like it." He hands me a flyer. I tuck it inside my textbook and then return my attention back to the teacher. Slowly his words are a little clearer, but it's still a struggle. I make it through the class with a slight headache, so I leave, needing to find the local coffee shop. It's a long line, but I manage to snag two medium caramel coffees before my next class and only get hit on twice more. I text my bestie and tell her where to meet me.

When I spot her, I wave the cups. "Good morning, Elsa," Angie cheers, running up to me in the middle of the quad. We hug and then I hand her a cup of coffee.

"Where's your posse of suits?"

"They are loosening the restrictions," I say.

"Yay," she cheers.

"I know, right?"

"You can finally hang out with me and meet some guys that I know."

"Sounds good, but not today. Two guys and one girl have already made passes at me today, and I'm not in the mood for more."

"That's because you're hot and that outfit is so cute."

"Thanks, but you're my friend and a bit biased." I wink at her.

"You got me," she says. "Besides, I'm trying to get in good so you can hook me up with your hot brother."

"Which one?" I already know which brother, but I want her to say it. She's been crushing on my brother since she met him.

"Milo, of course." She rolls her eyes and then takes a drink of her coffee.

My alarm goes off, reminding me that class starts in five minutes. "Oh shit. I got to go."

"I'll talk to you later, and maybe we can go out."

"Girl, I have class until tonight," I explain.

"Fine. Maybe tomorrow."

"Sounds good." I rush off to my next class.

By the time I finish my day, I'm so dang annoyed and tired. The boys are just as terrible as they were in high school. I swear last year wasn't this bad, but it's like they've realized I've sprouted tits and a personality finally. Not that I haven't looked this hot, but today I must be releasing some sort of pheromones.

At first there was my TA, followed by a bunch of new classmates that I've never met before, and as I'm walking out of my last class, I run into a former classmate who never spoke to me while we were in high school.

"Hey, Elsa. Girl, you're looking extra hot today. What's gotten into the water at your house?" Johnny Santos says. He eyes my backside with a twisted smirk like he's admiring my hard work in the gym.

"Shut up," I answer back.

"Don't be so mean, baby. I'm just giving you a compliment. You've gotten even hotter than last year, and your best friend told us you're finally off your parents' tight leash." Ugh, I could punch Angie in the tit when I see her. In fact, I'm making a note on my phone. Quickly, I whip it out and open up my task lists.

☐ **Punch Ange in the tit.**

I look up at him, displaying my annoyance, and say, "That doesn't mean I'm interested in dating guys who act like fools. Now excuse me." I scurry away and get in my car. It's the first time I'm allowed to drive myself to school without an entourage, but perhaps the old ways were better.

A sigh falls from my lips as I check my rearview mirror. My dad's usual security for me lingers two cars back, and I know that he didn't really give me full freedom, which I should have expected. A thought comes to me, and I wonder if Johnny was a test. Then again, maybe they purposefully put all these flirts in my way so I would want my old life back. Well, I passed and although the guys were obnoxious, I like having some freedom.

I didn't flirt back, and I didn't kill him, so I win. Sticking my tongue out in my rearview mirror, I drive out of my parking spot and through the lot. Johnny is standing with his friends by his car as I pass him, and he gives me a wave with a smirk. Ignoring him is the best thing I can do because there is no way I'm giving in to his bullshit.

When I get home, I'll give my dad an earful about his little test and then tell him that I can handle myself just fine and that I'm not going to be letting boys just scam on me. I still want my prince.

As I make my way through Vegas and toward our family estate, traffic is heavy, so it takes longer than expected. I turn up the tunes and let all the tension roll off my shoulders. By the time I pull through our gates and down our long driveway, all thoughts of arguing with my dad are out the window. I spot the familiar vehicle parked in his usual spot. Miles Ivanov is in my home. The dark prince. Could today get any more intense?

He always lingers in the back of my thoughts, lives in my dreams, in my diary, and in my heart, but he isn't my prince. At least several years older than me and a criminal mastermind, my godbrother Miles is talented and wanted by every woman in Vegas and back in Steeleville, where his parents live and where my mother is from.

I pull in alongside his vehicle, cutting off the engine, lingering in my seat and building up the courage to go inside. With my head down, I hear the front door open. Lifting my gaze, I spot my reason for staying back. It's Miles.

As soon as I step out of the car and walk to the portico, he says, "You're more than a few minutes late, Elsa."

"Excuse me? Since when are you my daddy?" I question, pressing my hands on my hips.

"I'm teasing, Princess," he says with a devilish smirk. "I wanted you to meet the new lady in my life." My heart drops into my stomach.

I swallow hard. "Why would—" I cut myself off before I say something stupid, and it's good because a cute little chocolate puppy comes running up to us yapping with a pretty pink collar around her neck. He scoops her up before she can run out the front door and then leads us inside the house like it's his home.

"Come inside. I don't want her to get out, Princess." He knows I hate when he calls me that. I don't really hate it, but I hate the way my body reacts to it. "I haven't picked a name for her yet. What do you think we should name her?"

"We?" My brows raise in what I'm sure is a comical way, especially because I catch my father quickly mask his expression, but I don't miss it. My teeth clench and still, I redirect my attention to Miles.

"Yes. Your dad offered your assistance in helping me care for this little girl," Miles says, scooping her up in his arms without any concern for his overly priced, well-tailored suit.

"You said you wanted some responsibility," my father adds, daring to speak after his betrayal.

"Yes, like a job. Not a puppy that's clearly not mine."

"Come, now, don't be mean. Just think of it as shared custody," Miles says, leaning in a little too close to me. Why does he smell so good? Even with a puppy in his arms, I can still smell his own personal scent. It's imprinted on my nostrils. I swear I can tell every time he's within breathing distance.

"Fine, but let me hold her," I huff, reaching out to grab her without invitation.

"Be careful. I'd hate for her to scratch you," he warns.

"It will be fine. She's a baby," I coo as I pull her from his arms. Our hands lightly touch, and I swear he intentionally lets them linger a little too long. That's surely not the case since he doesn't like me.

"What shall we name our baby?" he asks, petting her back, leaning in a little closer. She wags her tail, looking up at us with so much joy. I try not to like this feeling too much, so I create some emotional separation since he refuses to allow any physical kind.

"Hmm... that's a difficult one." I tap my chin. "Surely you can't give them one of your mistresses' names. We wouldn't want you to confuse them, so you'll have to think of something else."

He chuckles. "I love that sass, Princess. Any name you want because I have no mistresses."

My dad leans in and interjects, "Actually, Mistress would be good."

"It's perfect," I tease.

"I like it, too." He looks into my eyes, and for a moment I can't pull my gaze away.

"Come on. We need to have our meeting. Sweetheart, can you keep an eye on little Mistress for now?" Miles forces himself to step back.

I nod.

"Don't spoil our little girl too much."

"Please." I roll my eyes and scoff. "I'm sure your daddy is going to spoil you rotten," I say to the little puppy. A growl comes from behind me.

"We need to discuss some matters, Miles," my father insists.

"Yes," he answers, gives me one last look, and then walks away. I start playing with the little girl in my arms as the men's footsteps head down the hall.

"Maybe we can find her a master one day," I tease, forgetting myself for a moment. I don't think they heard me, but I'm wrong.

"One day," Miles says, closing my father's office door behind them.

I suck in a quick breath, grateful that they're already in his office so he couldn't hear or see me. "Okay, pretty girl. It's just you and me for now, so how about you and I get to know each other? But first I need to put my school things away and get a little more comfortable." It's late, and I haven't had dinner. I'm actually starving, since I'm pretty much running on coffee and a protein shake today.

I'm just passing by my father's office when I overhear Miles say, "What are we going to do about Elsa?" Miles says.

"I'm not sure. She's not..." Whatever they were going to say is cut off by Miles's phone ringing. What the hell are they talking about? I hear his unmistakable footsteps again, so I pick up my pace and rush toward the kitchen instead of my bedroom.

"Oh, sweetie, what do you have there?"

"Oh, this is one of Miles's mistresses. At least this one is pretty," I answer with a bit of attitude.

"I told you, Princess. I have no others. I've only had business dinners, and some of them happen to be female clients. One day you'll see," he says, stepping up behind me. Is he implying something between us? I can't handle him.

"I thought you were in a meeting," I challenge, wondering why he's bothering me after talking about me. I want to challenge him, but then I'd have to admit to eavesdropping.

"Something came up and I have to run."

"I bet."

"Why don't you run Mistress to my house and get her settled in with her things?"

"Because she's your bitch," I snap, feeling annoyed by the fact that he's running off suddenly.

"That's not nice talking about your baby like that. She's yours too." He scoffs and shakes his head. He whispers, "She didn't mean anything by that. She's just grumpy about school and she probably didn't eat all day." He bends down and kisses the top of her head and then smiles up at me so sweetly.

"I'm grumpy because you are…"

My mother cuts me off. "Elsa, would you like me to go with you and help?"

"That would be a great idea, Mrs. Martín," he adds, using his perfect charm as always. "I really must go. See you later."

"Mom, I'm going to change and then I'll be ready to take Mistress to his place."

"Did you really name her that?" she asks with her eyes wide.

"Yes. Dad is the one who came up with it after Miles said it was the only mistress he'd have, but I know he's full of shit. There's always a different name for his hookups."

"You sound jealous for someone who always protests that she doesn't like him." My mom is always telling me that, but I can't help denying my feelings. Miles is so much older and just wildly more mature than me.

"He's annoying."

"Yep. Handsome, rich, powerful, protective, and sweet, but yes, very annoying." She smiles and shakes her head.

I roll my eyes and take Mistress with me as we walk back out of the kitchen and then up the stairs toward my bedroom. Once inside, I set her down and finally kick off my shoes. "Your daddy is a major ass, but I'm sure you'll love him like every other female of any species."

She wags her tail happily like she already agrees. Damn—I knew it. He's already got her hooked. "Let me get changed, and don't you go messing up anything in my room or your daddy is going to pay." I point at her and scowl. She huffs and jumps on my bed, making herself comfortable, ducking her head into my pillow like she owns the place. She's just like Miles.

I don't take too long because I don't trust my new companion, but she's a good girl and is exactly where I left her, completely snuggled up on my bed like she's unwilling to move and it's her spot.

"Come on, girl. It's time to go and move in with your daddy."

She perks up and hops to her feet, wagging her tail. I snag her off the bed because I don't want her to jump and hurt herself.

When I get downstairs, my mother is ready to go, so we take the puppy outside to do her business before hopping into the SUV. I'd hate for her to do her business in the back of my mom's ride. Miles would get an earful when she saw him next along with a hefty cleaning bill.

"She's so precious, Elsa." My mother has fallen under her spell too. Honestly, so have I, and I wonder if that was Miles's plan all along. I wonder why he'd want me to look after his dog. He obviously doesn't have romantic feelings for me, so I bet my dad has something to do with it.

We arrive at Miles's property, which is only twenty minutes from ours, and the guards let us in. "Mrs. Martín, Miss Elsa, good evening," Carl says as we're welcomed into the front door of his estate. I love Miles's home, but it reminds me that one day he'll have a wife and family living here. A pang shoots through my chest at that image.

"Thank you. It's good to see you," my mother says with her perfect civility, but I just smile through the pain. They know I'm probably here under duress as usual. I've had to come here to drop off some documents that my father wanted to deliver, and once when my mom made a special treat for Miles. It was like I was their delivery service even though we had twenty other people they could have sent.

"Is this the new addition to the household?" Carl asks, staring down curiously at the cutie in my arms.

"Yes, meet Miles's Mistress."

"Elsa," my mother scolds.

"What? That's her name," I remind her.

"Her name is Mistress?" he asks.

"Yes, that's what we named her." He chuckles behind his hand.

"Very well. Everything is set up in the room off the stairs for her. Please come and see." He shows me, and Miles has gone all out for the little puppy.

"Wow. He took this new father thing to a whole new level."

"He's just practicing for the future," my mother says.

"What does that mean?" I ask her.

"Oh nothing. Just that a man like him will one day need a family to take over his empire."

"Oh, I suppose you are right about that." Again, there goes that pain in my chest. We look through all the puppy toys and on the shelf is the adoption paperwork. She's a chocolate labrador and her owners are Miles Ivanov and Elsa Martín. I shake my head and laugh.

"He really did make me part owner," I scoff, handing my mom the paper. She laughs.

"She's adorable though."

"She is." She jumps on my leg with her tail wagging, and I can't fight the smile she brings to my face. Miles might be a jerk, but I'm so happy to have her.

We get carried away playing with the puppy when Miles walks in. I see red on his collar, and I assume that he's a liar like most men. "She must have been worth dropping an important meeting for," I mutter under my breath.

"Sweetie, that's not lipstick," my mother says through clenched teeth. Then she smiles at Miles and gives him a motherly pat on his arm. "Miles, she's adorable. I think we should let you shower and change."

"Um, yes," he mumbles, and gives us a light wave before walking away. That was when I noticed his bandaged knuckles. That was blood on his collar.

"Oh my God, Mom. That was blood on his shirt. What do you think he went and did?" I stare after him as he disappears up the stairs.

My mother tugs me away and continues to scold me in a hushed tone, "I don't know, but it's none of your business, sweetheart."

"None of my business—what if he went and hurt somebody?" I let out a gasping whisper.

"Again, just none of our business, honey. More than likely that person deserves what they got. Miles is a good man. You know that, despite your anger toward him all the time." She's right; even when I'm cranky with him, I know the truth. I'm really never ever upset with him to the point that I don't think he's a good man, just an ass. I know what he's involved in. Maybe that is wrong; no, I know it's bad, but my father has been in the same situation.

In fact, he had helped him become the man he is. Miles's dad is a professional hacker and has taught Miles how to do so many things that he's an expert at being deceptive. I worry about how much he gets in trouble, but I don't imagine him being that dangerous. "Do you think it's his blood on his shirt?"

"I doubt it, sweetheart. Now, you're probably being a bit hysterical because you haven't eaten today. Let's get you some food on the way home." We do just that. Although I'm totally calmed down, I still wonder whose blood Miles had on his clothes.

CHAPTER FIVE

MILES

The second he closes the door, my future father-in-law says, "You are testing your luck today, Miles."

I chuckle because he's more than right. I'm pushing it, and I know it more than he does. The puppy is more for Elsa than for me. Hell, I didn't even know what kind of one to get. I asked the woman at the counter for her opinion. She had thirty questions that were twenty-nine too many. After I answered them I added that I wanted one that was good for a family as well. She recommended a labrador and our puppy was too cute to pass up. I had to pick one that would steal Elsa's heart. She loves dogs and I'd give her a dozen, but I don't want her to be overwhelmed when we start having babies.

The thought of putting a baby in Elsa's belly sounded so damn good to me. Sure, I'd wait, but the vision got me hard as hell. Another mark on her that she was mine. I couldn't deny that satisfied me to no end.

We never got to discuss that kiss, and I hadn't rectified my reaction because her father's health was more important. Since then, she's done everything to create a massive chasm between us. I'm not sure if it's like her brother said and it was truly an emotional mistake on her part, or if she's not sure about my feelings. Either way, I have to win her heart. The puppy is a start.

"Yes, well, it's been a rough day."

"With business, or Elsa?"

"Work has been easy in comparison. I hadn't realized how agitated I'd be worrying about her safety all day."

"Her safety, or all the guys her age full of testosterone looking at her?" he says. He's so damn lucky that I respect him. "I'm just pointing out the truth. As a man obsessed with his wife for the past twenty-five years, I assure you I understand. Give it some time, and don't deviate from your plan. You're not a man who buckles under pressure."

"You're right. Thanks for the reminder."

"Are there problems other than my defiant daughter who wants to catch criminals?" he asks.

"There are just so many more risks with all those people on campus. I'm not sure if the other families can get to her if she's not careful. Now we've decided to give her a little space, and I don't think it's a good idea."

"I'm sure she's fine. Have you had any whispers about them over the summer?"

"No, but she's hardly left the house and now she's back into the world. They are waiting for a moment of weakness, and we've just opened her up to an attack," I remind him. I'm not going to let a soul touch her. Not after her sweet lips grazed mine and if I'd been in my right mind, I would have crushed her mouth that day, but it was smart that I backed off.

I run my hands through my hair, thinking about my woman and my need to hold her. "What are we going to do about Elsa?"

"I'm not sure. She's not…"

I raise my hand, stopping the conversation between us. Seeing that it's the man I had on Elsa today, I know it's extremely important. She thought it was her security that was farther back, but I had a guy that looked like a student much closer. "I have to take this call."

Taking a deep breath, I answer as calmly as possible. After all, she was in the other room, looking rather annoyed with me, but still unharmed. "What is it?"

"Boss, there was this little fucker who was talking to your girl just as she was getting ready to leave campus."

"What do you mean he was talking to my girl?" The words slip past my lips as if they were deadly shards. I don't care if her father hears me because I'm about to lose it.

"He was getting a little fresh outside her last class."

"Did you see what happened?"

"Yeah, but you told us to stay back and not do anything unless something happens. She looked really upset, but she pushed his hand away from her face."

"He fucking touched her?" My voice bellows through the room.

"Yeah, but he didn't hurt her."

Another man putting his hands on Elsa sends violent thoughts straight to the forefront of my mind. All the ways I wanted to destroy this bastard danced in my head. "I didn't ask that. He put his hands on my fucking woman."

"Yeah, it looked like he was trying to flirt hard. They seem to have known each other."

"Do you know who this fucker was?" He had better have the right answer for me or he was going to face my wrath first.

"At first I didn't, but I pulled his plates. They belong to Antonio Santos."

I cut him off because I'm sure that it couldn't have been that old bastard. "I know that old fucker wasn't trying to hit on my girl."

"No. He has a son that's about her age, so I pulled up his driver's license and it's him, Johnny Santos. What do you want us to do?"

"I need to have a word with that little shit. Find out where he is." I end the call and turn to my future father-in-law.

He understood the entire conversation without having to hear the other half.

"So who is this guy?"

"Johnny Santos. I got to go." We both knew the ramifications of a negative encounter. Santos crossed a line whether he knew it or not.

"Do you need my help?" my godfather asks.

"Not unless I have a problem with the father later, but you warned these motherfuckers before. I won't be taking this lightly. She's mine, and if he wants to play stupid games, he can win a motherfucking stupid prize."

"Calm down, son. You know she's not going to like you doing this."

"But you know I have to," I remind him.

"You're right, because he stepped out of line and he knows it. Just let me know if you need anything, and once you're done, we're going to need to talk about this whole 'your girl' thing since things aren't solidified between you two," he says with a chuckle.

I nod and leave his office. After a brief visit in the kitchen with Elsa and her mom, I say goodbye to the dog. Quickly, I slide into my SUV with two of my security team members to go meet with the little shit who happens to not be hanging out at home where he should be. He's either got to be a fucking fool, or has got brass balls because he fucked up today and needs a lesson.

I find him outside a skate park, smoking and drinking like a fucking jerkoff. "Santos, a word," I state calmly over the din around me. He looks up at me, and his face freezes before he catches himself and tries to act cool. I'm sure his father would love it. I'm betting he's unaware that he violated our understanding.

"What's up?" he answers with more bravado than he'll soon have. He's surrounded by some of his goons, some little pussies and a couple chicks making him feel tougher than he really is.

"You heard me—get the fuck over here right now before we have a bigger problem."

"Hold my beer. I have to talk to the old guy." Yeah, that attitude is going to get him hurt really fast.

"He's hot. He's giving me daddy vibes," the girl next to him utters, licking her lips. Daddy vibes? I'm twenty-four.

"Don't bother, sugar. Rumor has it that the big, bad casino owner likes twinks." I ignore his gay remark because I've heard the speculation recently, not that it matters. I'm wondering who would spread the rumors when the families at the meeting had been aware of my sentiments.

When it comes to my sexuality, the only person whose opinion I care about is Elsa's, and she thinks I'm sleeping with the woman I am spotted with every once in a blue moon. Those were always business deals. Nothing more. Ever.

Before I was interested in her, I'd been too busy to focus on dating. It wasn't that I hadn't considered it, but it requires effort that I have no interest in investing energy into. Since I've realized my feelings for Elsa, no one else even catches my attention for a fraction of a second.

"Did you, or did you not, touch Elsa today?" I ask.

"What the fuck does it matter?" he spits back.

"I swear you're either dumb as fuck, or you have a serious thrill issue. I'll only ask you once more, but you're not going to like the result. Did you touch Elsa?"

"She's fucking fair game." My fist lands directly on his cute face, sending him onto his ass with blood spurting everywhere.

"She isn't to be touched. You've been warned. It's the last warning you'll get. Next time it will be something other than my fist that meets your face."

"You fucking pussy. What did you do?" he shouts, but it comes out pretty weak since he's holding his nose as his boys attempt to look tough. My guys reach for their pieces, but I raise my hand.

"I should cut out your tongue," I snarl as he tries to steady himself on his elbow. I continue, "but I don't have time for a war with your father over your pathetic life. However, cross me again, and I'll make time."

I don't allow him to say another word before I walk away. My men follow after giving them a quick scare. "We're always watching," Kyros warns him.

I drive back to the house, pissed that my fucking knuckles are busted from hitting that fucker. Luckily, we keep a first aid kit in the car and wrap my hand up quickly. Maybe I should have beat his ass until he was unable to walk. His father had been given the warning just a few months ago. They hadn't taken me seriously, but they found out today I mean business.

CHAPTER SIX

ELSA

LITTLE MISTRESS AND I HAVE BEEN GETTING ALONG WELL, BUT it's time for school again. I stayed in and did my online class before receiving a message from Miles to remind me to walk Mistress.

ME

Don't you have people there that can let her out?

MISTRESS'S DADDY

Yes, but she likes you.

ME

Fine.

I drive over to Miles's estate to walk Mistress, and Carl smirks and shakes his head. He's probably thinking the same thing I am. Why am I here or why are they here?

Then again, maybe they don't like taking care of a pet on top of their regular duties.

"Apparently, you all are incapable of walking this little princess," I muttered, sounding more annoyed than I really am. Other than having to see a man who drives my heart insane, I don't mind playing with Mistress. She makes me happy.

"Yes, she's a wild beast that you can only tame," Carl teases. "Would you like lunch?"

"I'd love it."

"Sit in the garden with the little Mistress and I'll have it brought out."

"Great, thank you," I say, smiling as I pat my thigh to summon Mistress who is running around in circles.

I eat my wonderful chicken salad and drink my tea while Mistress lies at my feet. Once I'm done, I get another text from Miles.

Did you enjoy your meal?

Yes. Carl knows how to treat a lady.

Carl does what I tell him.

Whatever. I have to go home and do some homework.

See you tomorrow.

> I can't do it tomorrow. I have class until six and then I have a study session, so I'll be busy.

Fine. See you Thursday for the custody exchange.

> With pleasure.

WEDNESDAY MORNING ISN'T AS DIFFICULT AS MONDAY, BUT I'm still struggling with my professor's accent. At the end of class, I inform the TA that I'll be coming tonight to the skull session because I need it.

"That's good. We should have a handful of students tonight."

"Thanks." I leave and walk around to get my coffee, but the line is too long so I forgo the extra jolt I need. "Good morning, bestie," Angie says, walking up to me with her coffee in hand.

"Morning. What do you have to drink?" I question.

"My usual latte. Wanna sip?" she asks, holding it out for me.

"Sure," I take it from her with my non-dominant hand, and then I slug her in the tit.

"Ow. What the fuck was that for?" she hisses, pressing her hand to her chest, rubbing the spot like I got her good.

"You told Johnny Santos I was available, and he is slimy."

"Well, it's not like it's a lie. Jeez, you're a dick. Give me back my coffee. You don't deserve my caffeine goodness." She snatches it back and huffs.

"It's cool because I already had my coffee." I stick out my tongue. I did, but I could use another three cups.

"Yeah, and you could have three more before the day's out," she adds. Damn, she knows me too well.

I laugh and nod. "You got me there."

"Besides, why is it so bad? You can get gorgeous, wealthy men after you besides Miles, who is clearly a god that wants to make you his goddess." She rolls her eyes dramatically.

She's been saying that all summer, but I tell her she's nuts every time. "You're crazy. He's just my controlling godbrother who helps monitor me like the rest." Up until recently I hadn't seen Miles, so there is no doubt he doesn't want me. It's only because of my father's surgery that he's taken a more active role in my protection. "Whatever."

"I have to get back to my next class. I don't want them to find out I ditched a class."

"You're nineteen, and you still have your parents hounding you?" She doesn't know what it's like to be in my position because her parents aren't insanely wealthy or powerful. It comes with more threats than normal, which my parents know from firsthand experience. Their worries are legitimate, so they're extremely protective. If they even thought for a second that I wasn't where I was supposed to be, they'd think I was abducted.

"Can you go out this weekend?"

"Why not before then?"

"Because I have to work and besides, I want to go to a party this weekend."

"Oh, well, I'll have to see. My mom has her annual charity event, so I probably have to lend her a hand, so let me know when it is."

"Oh, that's right. Well, give your mom my love. She's an angel."

"That she is." A damn crazy angel. Everyone thinks my dad is insane, but my mother is just as crazy, and they are perfect for each other.

I finish the rest of my classes, and it's time to finally head home.

My phone vibrates, and then I remember I'm not leaving just yet. I have a study session. What did I get myself into? Maybe this will be a one-time thing.

I go to my car and drop off the rest of my things, taking only what I need. Heading to the library, I go in and see the small group with the TA at the head of the wooden rectangle table.

"Hey, Elsa, come have a seat." Surprisingly there is an open seat next to him, even though there are five other students already there.

"We're glad you could make it." I recognize, like, two of the kids, but there are so many in the class that I can't say they're not all in the same session. It doesn't matter because the study session goes on way too long, and I decide that I'm not going again.

My security lurks in the distance as I walk to my car. It's late, so I'm grateful that they're nearby. I call my mom and let her know I'm on my way home.

THE CHARITY EVENT GOES OFF WITHOUT A HITCH, AS USUAL, and my mother hardly needs my help, but I'm there to be her moral support as she runs the food and clothing drive. Once it's over, I'm tired, so I go straight home to take a shower and find something to eat before bed. Everything can wait until tomorrow.

A text pops up on my dashboard screen as I drive home.

ANGE

> Girl, heard your boyfriend went ape shit on Johnny. Beat his ass and told him to stay away from you.

I tap my steering wheel and voice reply back to Ange.

> No way. Where did you hear that?

> Some of the girls at this party I'm at.

> You're at a party? You didn't tell me you were going to a party.

> You said you had something with your mom. Can you come out now?

>> I'm tired. Let me know if you find out anything else.

ANGE

> Okay lame. See you Monday at school.

As I pull into my spot in the driveway, I think about when Miles walked in with that splatter of blood on his collar. It was probably Johnny's. Would any guy get in trouble for talking to me, or was it Johnny's disrespect? The bastard has the nerve to interfere in my relationships when he wants nothing to do with me.

I plan to give him a piece of my mind, so I call his cell but get no answer.

I send a message to Miles.

>> I don't know why you beat up Johnny, but it's not cool. Stay out of my personal life.

> Contact changed to "Mistress's Bad Daddy"

> Not going to happen. It's my job to protect you from scum, and Johnny knows his damn place. He was warned before that you were off-limits.

>> Off-limits? I'm only off-limits to who I want to be. I don't need your dating assistance.

> Actually, you do.

I call him, but he refuses to take my calls, so I call his office and his assistant answers. "I'm sorry, Mr. Ivanov is currently out of town and will not be back until tomorrow night."

"Thank you." I toss my phone onto the nightstand and then go to take a shower.

Where has he gone? It pisses me off that he can come and go as he pleases, but he controls my life. The bastard.

My drive to Miles' estate is uneventful as expected, and I'm not even stopped at the gate like usual. I suppose since he's not here, there's no worry that I'll accidentally run into one of his women. They open up for me, and I'm allowed in. As I exit the vehicle, the doors open and the little Mistress jumps out the front door yapping and wagging her tail.

"Whoa, relax, baby girl. Give your mommy some breathing room," Miles says. I gasp as I take him in. He's standing there in just a pair of gym shorts, chest bare and sweat glistening over his perfectly sculpted muscles. Why does he have to be so amazing, and I'm just the girl he shunned?

"Maybe Daddy should take the same advice," I reply with pursed lips. He isn't supposed to be here until tomorrow night.

"Why do you hate me so much?"

"You weren't supposed to be here," I state. He takes the few steps down his stone porch, closing the small distance between us and forcing me to take a step or two back, but then Mistress runs behind me. I lose my footing, but Miles is quick, and he has me in his arms, holding me firmly to his chest.

"Are you okay?" he asks, his fingers brushing the loose strands of hair behind my ear.

"Yes, but is Mistress?"

"Look," he chuckles and smirks. She is jumping after a butterfly.

"Good, I would have been devastated to have crushed her."

"Then maybe you shouldn't run away from me." The deep rumble in his chest sends shockwaves of desire and confusion through me.

"Maybe you shouldn't be chasing me?" What am I saying? I want this man chasing me, craving me like I crave him.

"That's like telling Icarus to stop flying toward the sun. Not going to happen."

"You've lost it. Did you work out too hard?"

"No—"

"Sir, you have a call. It's Miss Steiner." There is the reminder I need that I'm not the one for him, and he's not the one for me.

"Thank you," he grunts to Carl, clearly annoyed that he interrupted us. "I need to shower. Can you take care of the little girl here?"

"You have a staff, and you don't need me here for that." I want to tell him that Miss Steiner can care for his dog since he's handing her his private number, but I control myself.

"I know, but I'd like you to help with her."

"Fine," I huff. He turns around without another word and goes inside, leaving me with the exuberant puppy. We run around outside for a little longer before she gets tired, and then we stroll inside.

I spend two hours in his house lounging about with Mistress while enjoying the luxury as if I don't have the same thing, but there is something warm about his place. "Come on, girl. Let's go raid his library. I don't know where your daddy went, but I'm getting bored." I wonder if he went out on a date and just left us here without any notice.

We roam over to the library and push the door open to find Miles reading a book. "Are you freaking serious right now?"

"What?" he asks, lowering his book.

"I'm here watching your dog, and you're here just chilling out."

He shrugs. "I'm actually spending some time in my house. I never said I was leaving after my shower. You're the one who assumed that."

"Well, since you're home, I have to go. Besides, she's fine and can spend time by herself."

"Sit with me, Elsa."

"Why?"

"Because I want you to."

"What if I don't?" He grabs my hand and drags me down to his side on the sofa. I plop down, and my heart can't handle being this close to him. Why am I so flustered being this close? Because the last time we were this close, I made a fucking fool of myself. He looked mortified.

"Tough."

"Miles," I whine.

"Yes, Elsa." The way he says my name sends a delightful tingle through my body, and it's all wrong. It's how I ended up against him, embarrassing myself.

"I need to go. I have a test to study for," I blurt out as I jump off the sofa.

He sighs and then nods. "Be careful, and we'll talk about this living arrangement later."

"Fine." I'm not even sure how we came to share a dog, but Mistress is his, not mine. Even as I say that, I don't believe it anymore.

The next morning, I go to school and see Johnny; he avoids me completely. "Stay away from me, Elsa." I don't miss the black eyes that are healing along with the small bandage on his nose. His eyes widen, and that's when I spot my father's security team nearby.

"No problem, Johnny." I walk away without another word to anyone. After my classes, I'm having a major sit down with my father. He has to call off his hound dog. Even if

Johnny's family is in the mafia, I'll shut the situation down so he has no reason to get involved.

My mind isn't on my schoolwork at all. I can't make it through any classes, so it's a merciful blessing that they have canceled my last class.

I drive to the hotel and go up to my father's office. He's in a meeting with my brother, but their assistant allows me in. Thankfully, Miles is at the casino, and I don't have to see him because I don't have the nerve to face him right now.

The assistant barely opens the door before I barge in and close it behind him. "Please excuse her. Someone forgot her manners today," my brother apologizes for me.

"What's on your volatile mind, Princess?"

"Your guard dog needs to back off."

"What guard dog? All of your security has kept their distance."

"Miles. He's… he's…" I blush because I can't describe why I'm so damn pissed without giving myself away.

"He's what?"

"He's sticking his nose where it doesn't belong."

"What do you mean? Is he harassing you? Do you not like him?" My face heats and turns completely red.

"Sweetheart, do you want to tell me what's going on between you and Miles?"

"Nothing, Daddy." Other than he broke my heart without even trying and he won't allow me to get over it. It's a perpetual vicious cycle.

"Why are you lying, baby?"

"I'm not lying."

"You have been upset with him for a long time. You come in here spitting fire because he's bothering you. Now, I know you're crazy about him, so I don't understand why you're so upset with him. Has he hurt you?"

"No, of course not. It's nothing like that."

"If you're not going to tell him the truth, I am."

"What's going on, Son?"

"The day you were in the hospital having your surgery, she kissed Miles."

"What?"

"Yeah. And he didn't kiss her back. He froze like a damn statue."

"Oh."

"Yeah."

"So what's the point in liking somebody who doesn't like you back? So I don't need your guard dog protecting me all the time, Daddy. It's hard enough to have a crush on somebody and then to have them around all the time when they don't like you, but then I already made a fool of myself. Then he goes and beats up guys that do like me."

"Els, just because he didn't kiss you there? Come on— what did you expect him to do? Toss you on the ground in the middle of the waiting room? The man is trying to be respectful at a time where you were grieving and scared. Taking advantage of you wasn't the right thing to do."

"He's right, sweetheart. Miles's feelings for you are real, baby. His protection is more than just at my request. He told me himself. When it comes to beating up Santos, he had his reasons, and he'll do much worse if Santos ever approaches you again, so don't argue with any of us on that."

"Are you serious?"

"About Santos? Deadly."

"I'm talking about Miles."

"Of course. He's crazy about you."

"Do you think I pushed him too far?"

"I was told you were here," Miles growls from the doorway.

Milo walks up to Miles and says, "You hurt my sister, and all bonds we have are cut."

"Understood, but first I need to have a talk with this crazy woman. She and I have a lot to clear up." He walks right up to me and his mouth lands on mine. I freeze, stunned because my father and brother are right there.

"Damn, we're zero for two," he teases as he pulls back.

"Maybe not try kissing in front of me, dickhead."

"I just wanted her to see what it was like to be stunned." He looks at me right in the eyes. "Now come on, princess. You and I have a lot to discuss, and our baby girl needs a walk."

"I'll be working from home tomorrow morning, and we can discuss matters tomorrow evening at my home over dinner," Miles says, leading me from the office, and no one says another word. I'm actually still so shocked by everything that I move with him and don't even open my mouth until we're outside the room.

CHAPTER SEVEN

MILES

I HAVE A LOT OF THINGS TO DO BEFORE I HEAD HOME, including a visit from the jeweler with Elsa's ring. I've spent a long time deciding what it would be. After all the years we've known each other, I want it to be special, but with Vegas, nothing seems to be that way. Everything here is gaudy, extravagant, way over the top. No matter what I see or think of, I feel like I'm just throwing my money around. None of it shows the depth of my obsession.

This piece is it, though. I've worked hard on it, and it incorporates everything she likes, from her favorite flower, to her favorite books, to her love of dogs.

I close the app after a few moments and return to my business matters that require my attention. It takes more time than I expect, even leaving the jeweler waiting in my personal lobby to be received.

"My apologies," I say.

"No, no. It is my fault for arriving too early." The level of fear I bring is well known, and he doesn't want to disappoint.

"Please come and show me what you've brought me." He nods and sets the suitcase on the table beside my desk. Opening it, he lays out the cloth and then unveils the three-carat pink diamond tear-drop stone with chocolate diamonds surrounding it. Etched inside, I inscribed a message for her, and it's perfect. A *dark prince loves his princess.*

Elsa always believed in fairytales and love, wanting to marry a prince. She doesn't see me like that, but I'll be whatever she needs because my life doesn't exist without her in it.

"It's perfect, Mr. Greenberg," I state, sending the payment through. He wipes the ring down and places it in the special box before handing it to me.

"She is one lucky woman."

"I am the lucky one."

"Then you are blessed, Sir."

"That I am." I escort him out with a handshake before closing the door. Pressing the box to my chest, I take a deep breath and send up a silent prayer that I don't ruin this because I'm not above kidnaping a princess.

With the ring in my pocket, I prepare to leave for the day. It's finally time to claim the woman I am in love with. She has revealed her hand. I know she loves me, and this time I'm not going to let her worm her way out of my grasp. I don't care what threat is in the way because I'll tear anyone down that gets between us.

There is a quick knock on my office door. "Mr. Ivanov, Miss Martín just entered the hotel alone and she wasn't happy."

"Okay. I'm on my way." I storm up there to hear the tail end of the conversation. So my little beauty is still quite upset by our kiss. I couldn't believe that she hadn't seen past my ruse with Mistress and the stupid attempts to get her in my home, to like it and want to stay.

I've been bold as fuck right in front of her father and older brother, but I don't care. I'm done waiting, and she needs to understand how much she means to me.

Elsa stops me, tugging my arm outside the private elevators. "Where are we going?"

"Home."

"Home?" she repeats with a questioning smile spreading across her flushed face.

I cup her warmed cheek. "Yes. We never talked about the living arrangements. I'm getting tired of you going back and forth."

"Oh, are you?" She adds an audaciously raised brow to the look, and my cock loves the boldness.

"Yes, you know Mistress misses you," I say, leading her inside and then turning to the control panel.

"What about you?"

I shrug. "She doesn't miss me at all."

She glares at me. "You're an ass. I mean, do you miss me when I leave?"

"Every second that I'm not with you, Elsa." Sliding the key into the lock, I shut down the elevator, which turns off the cameras. My hand cups her face and I say, "I'm going to kiss you, Elsa."

"Please," she whispers. Our lips connect, and it's magnetic. I lean in and push her against the elevator wall, sliding my tongue along the seam of her lips until she parts them. Diving in, I taste her tongue, sliding mine against hers.

"Miles," she whispers, panting so wonderfully. My phone vibrates in my slacks, and I know damn well who it is without having to check it. Her father is giving me a fucking warning to cut it out. I have to pull away before her father switches on the cameras. Dragging myself back, I release my hold and twist the key before pulling it from the lock.

"Later, Princess. Your dad has access to the cameras, too. I don't need them trying to kill me before we're married and my baby is growing inside you."

"Baby?" she asks so softly that her voice cracks. I'm not sure if that's a positive or negative response, so we need to have a talk before we take the bedroom talk any further.

"Yes. I know you're probably not ready." She presses her fingers to my lips.

"There is so much we need to talk about, but, Mr. Ivanov, this isn't the place for the conversation." She lifts her gaze to the camera light above. I nod, face forward, and take her hand in mine. The door opens, and we exit. I lead her to my waiting vehicle. Kyros holds the back door for us, and she slides in first. I watch her greedily as she moves her delectable body.

"Are you staring at my backside, Miles?" That saucy tone does nothing to stem the growing desire I have inside me. We're not going to make it long before we end up in bed. It's not what I want, even though my hunger to fuck her is there.

"Yes, I am," I answer without an ounce of shame. I want her naked, but I should take her out first. The dog will keep us distracted, so I can behave like a damn civilized human instead of the damn animal I want to be.

She doesn't say a word, but the look and smile that spreads to her eyes says it all.

"I hope you enjoyed the view."

"I did, very much." I smirk and then close the door behind us. Sitting next to her with the right to touch Elsa has never felt so good. Looking toward my driver and head of security, I say, "Kyros, take us to my home, please."

"We've been in the car together before, but this feels different," Elsa admits with a soft sigh.

"Yes, it does. I can hold you and stare at you and not feel guilty. I don't have to sneak glances, hide my longing from you."

"Why didn't you just tell me? Goodness, when did you start having these feelings?"

"When you came crashing into the room, summoning your father to see the doctor. Truthfully, I noticed you before, but I thought I was imagining the attraction. Then, you landed in my arms, and nothing could change the path I was on."

"Then why did you take the long path? That was four months ago."

"Your dad was recovering; I wasn't trying to send the man back into the hospital. Besides, I needed to keep you safe from the other families without the distraction of having you in my bed."

"And now I'm safe?"

"I can't say with one hundred percent certainty that they'll back off, but I laid into Johnny, and maybe they saw how serious I was."

"I believe so. We saw each other at school, and he refused to even speak to me."

"That's fucking good because I gave him a gentle warning to stay away."

"Did you have to hit him in the first place?"

"Yes. He'd been warned before that day, and he hadn't listened."

"Oh." She bites down on her pretty bottom lip. The vehicle comes to a stop, and my gate opens. We don't say a word as we pull up to the front of the house. I can sense she's nervous, and I can't deny that I'm almost as worried as aroused. Fucking this up isn't an option.

As much as I want to walk through the doors and carry her straight to our bedroom, we need to straighten out our relationship before I lose my head.

"Princess, let's go inside." I step out and take her hand, leading her inside where Carl smiles as Mistress runs out and jumps up my leg and then to Elsa as soon as she spots her. "Look—Mommy is home where she belongs, Mistress." I bend down and pet the little puppy, earning excited tail wags and a couple hand licks.

"Should we take her for a walk?"

"Sounds like a good idea."

"Carl, we'll be having the Martín family over for dinner."

"Yes, Sir. I'll have dinner prepared by six. I'm glad to see you're here, Elsa."

"Thank you, Carl."

"Yes, thank you. We're going to take Mistress for a walk in the garden."

"Yes, Sir." He leaves us and we walk to the back and Mistress follows with her tiny paws and eager tail. Elsa runs after her and giggles so adorably. She drops to her butt and then tucks her legs under her hips, letting the dog run to her. They play together while I remove my suit jacket and set it on the patio chair, and then I grab some of her toys in the bin by the side of the house.

"Mistress, come here." I squeeze the toy, and she comes running.

"She's so fickle, isn't she?"

"She loves her toys."

"I think she loves you."

"What's not to love?" I tease.

"Let me get back to you on that," she answers with a smirk before getting up off the ground. I swoop her up before she's fully standing.

"What did you say, Princess?" I tickle her waist.

"Nothing. I swear." She giggles and then Mistress comes to her defense, yelping at my feet. "Don't worry, baby girl. Daddy's not hurting Mommy."

"Not yet. Mommy's going to be yelling Daddy's name tonight."

"Not sooner?"

"No. As much as I want to spread you out like a meal and then fill you up so deep, I don't want your parents to arrive before we've finished."

"Oh."

"Yes, oh."

"How am I going to stay here without my things?"

"Since you don't go back to school until Monday, we'll go back tomorrow and get your clothes."

"But there is something that's yours." I drop down to one knee. "Elsa, I'm in love with you, and thankfully it didn't take me too long to realize it. I'm so grateful I didn't realize it sooner. What I'm saying is…will you marry me?"

"I think you're a little late…"

"Woman…okay, I'm answering it for you. We already have a little puppy together. It's a sealed deal. Enough said." I slide the ring on her finger and then pull her in for a kiss.

"I suppose since we do share custody, it's probably for the best." The smile on her face couldn't be wider.

"I love you, Elsa." She kisses my chin and then my lips tenderly until we're lost in each other's arms.

A low yelping yawn comes from my feet, and I look down to see our puppy curling between us. "Looks like someone is tired."

"Yes, it does."

"Let's take her inside and wash up." She picks up the sleepy pup, and I press my hand to the small of her back as we walk back inside. We wash our hands, and then I lead her into the family room. "Would you like something to drink?"

"No, thank you."

"So, I need you to understand something, Elsa."

"What is it?"

"I want us to be together, and I'm not just talking about dating. I'm looking forward to forever with you. I understand that you have dreams to be a forensic scientist."

"Are you…"

"Hold on. I'm not trying to stop you from becoming one. Not at all. I'm just saying there may be some bumps in the road along the way."

"What's that supposed to mean?"

"Well, one, we'll be getting married, so the wedding and honeymoon will happen, and I'm not sure if that will interfere. Then, there's the chance that we have a baby in the next couple of years."

"How many babies?" she asks with bright, wide eyes.

"I don't know. It depends on how many babies we can handle. I'm running a hotel and casino with your brothers while I plan on giving you the rest of my time. Maybe starting a family right away might not be the best idea."

"My mother put me on birth control at the beginning of the summer."

"Oh yeah?"

"Yes. She said it would be a good idea until I finished school."

"Well, then, it's good because we have time for each other and you can finish school." I pull her into my arms, tipping her face upward with my hand under her chin. "Now that we have that squared away, my beautiful Elsa, I need to taste these lips again."

She closes her eyes, waiting for me to claim her soft pink lips. I lean in and close my mouth over hers, sliding a hand into her hair, cupping the back of her neck to bring her face close to mine. Our mouths angle sideways as we deepen the kiss, moans falling from our lips.

Carl coughs, interrupting us. "Sir, Mr. and Mrs. Martín have arrived."

"Please escort them in here."

When they finally enter the family room, I smile proudly and greet them, "Thank you for coming."

"Of course. We can't miss a wonderful dinner and a chance to see our daughter before you steal her away from us so unexpectedly," her father adds with a look of annoyance.

"I thought it would have been obvious after everything that we discussed."

"I don't believe we discussed her just moving in with you." He steps closer, his anger becoming more obvious.

Mrs. Martín steps up and presses her hand to his chest. "Come, now, Emiliano. You know very well that the second you had me in your grasp, I was living with you."

"You are correct, my love. This is different—she's my daughter."

Mrs. Martín laughs, and he turns to look at her with a scowl. "You are being ridiculous. I told you before that this was happening, and you didn't listen to me."

She walks up to Elsa with a small pink and white bag. "Sweetheart, I packed you an overnight bag. I'm sure you'll gather more of your things later."

"Thank you." She takes it and sets it aside.

"Dinner is ready," Carl says. We all go into the dining room and take our seats with Elsa at my right.

"Everything smells wonderful."

"Thank you, Mrs. Martín. I'll tell the chef that."

"Where is the rest of the family?" Elsa asks, looking at her parents.

"They had other matters to attend to, and unfortunately as you know Milo is away on business and won't be back until next week."

"Well, I'm glad you could make it," I state, knowing that he wasn't too pleased with me.

"So what are your plans? Are you going to be living with my daughter without getting married?"

"No," Elsa and I blurt out at the same time. I laugh.

"I'm glad you feel that way, Elsa, because we're getting married as soon as possible."

"Oh, really? How soon are you talking about? Are you planning to start a family?"

"We're going to wait some time before we start on grandchildren, but I'd like to marry fast. I don't see a point in waiting."

"Maybe take some time to get to know each other," Emiliano says.

"I've known her since we were kids. Yes, there are the little things we don't know, but I know she loves Mexican and Chinese, but hates pasta even though she loves going to Italy. Her favorite books are crime novels from the past, like nineties and early two-thousands."

Elsa twisted her head with her mouth wide open. "I can't believe you know that."

"Yeah, I noticed it on your reading account online. You have an addiction to some of the older books from those times before technology got out of control and so much of the market was overly saturated."

"So when is the wedding?"

"We live in Vegas," Elsa offers.

"Elsa, we can get married in a lavish wedding if you want, but I want to start planning it now and have it ready within the next six months. No need to wait any longer. Hell, other than the dress and the invites, we have access to everything else at our fingertips easily."

"The dress? Do you think that would be hard?" she asks me.

"No, but I'm not sure where you want to get it or how long it takes to make. Don't pretend the princess doesn't want her picture-perfect wedding."

"I do."

"Then you'll get it."

"Three months should be plenty."

"Good. We need to start right away." Her mother rubs her hands together with excitement.

"I'll send you the calendar for the hotel and then general group schedule for the families, and we'll see if there's any major conflicts."

"Thanks, Dad."

"Thanks."

After they leave, I escort Elsa to our bedroom, taking her bag with us. "This is our bedroom."

"I'm not going to have my own bedroom until we're married?" she asks with a flat expression.

"Are you fucking serious?"

"No, but you should see the look on your face. It's priceless." She opens her bag and starts pulling things out onto the dresser. The thought of her things everywhere feels just right. I'd already cleared out space in the room, added an additional dresser, and ordered the same hygiene products she uses at home.

"We'll see how you're looking when I'm buried balls deep inside you and you're creaming all around me."

"Let's see if you can make me come."

"I'm going to do my best, no matter how many tries it takes."

"No one could call you a quitter, Miles. Luckily, no one knows this side of me. Can I take a shower?"

"Absolutely. Your usuals should be there. I hope they're the right kind, or I'm going to have to kick someone's ass."

She walks into the bathroom and looks for a moment before peeking at me with a devilish smile. "I can't believe you did all this. Then again, now that I know the truth, I suppose it's right up your alley."

"Up my alley? What's that supposed to mean?"

"You're the kind to leave nothing to chance or not taken care of. I'm surprised my clothes weren't already here."

"I hadn't expected this to happen so soon. I was planning on giving you a little more time before convincing you that we needed to give us a chance."

"Then I'm glad I threw a fit and got my way."

"I think I'm the one who got my way."

"I'd say it was a win-win." She winks and then closes the door. As the shower turns on, I have to fight the instant arousal, so I quickly shower in a guest bedroom and change into my pajama bottoms. She's still showering, so I do some work on my phone until she's done. Elsa finally comes out in just a towel; my tongue nearly falls onto the floor.

"Why, Princess, it's like you're begging to be fucked tonight."

"Is it that obvious?" Her eyes aren't focused on my face at all. They're laser focused on my chest and abs. Damn— now I'm grateful that I focus on my diet and exercise. I want her tongue licking me from my chest to my balls, and from the look on her face, I wonder if she's got that same idea. Her tongue peeks out, and my dick jerks in my pajamas.

"No. Not at all." I drag her to me and crush her mouth in a hard, rough kiss. "But as it happens, I'm a very intuitive man." My tongue slides down to her jaw, and then I scrape my teeth along her pulse.

"Oh my goodness. This feels so good."

"Damn. I'm totally going to defile you tonight."

"Please do. Show me what you can do to make me come so hard that I need more and more."

"Challenge accepted, Princess." I tug her towel and stare at her perfect set of tits that has me salivating. I bend my knees and then scoop her up and carry her to bed. She lets out a shriek before giggling. I drop her onto the mattress, watching her sexy curves jiggle.

I follow after her, leaning my body over hers. "I need to be inside you right now."

"What are you waiting for?"

"I need to get you ready. There's no way this is going to work like this."

"Why? I'm so horny." I slide my fingers down her perfectly taut stomach that won't always be that way. I want to lick my way there, but I have to be patient. Fuck, waiting wasn't a burden until now.

I lift my finger and suck on it until it's drenched and then run it over her wet, hot pussy. She may be aroused, but my beautiful woman isn't where either of us need her to be.

I rub her slit, and her hips buck off the mattress. "Fuck, Miles."

"That's it, baby. Let me feel how horny you are, but you need to calm down and let me in." I start to push my finger in, and it's so damn tight my finger is struggling. She gasps.

"Oh my."

"Yes, that's just one finger." I pump my middle finger while my thumb massages her clit. "Relax for me." I lean over and kiss my woman and then add a second finger. She continues to calm down and open up for me. I pull out my fingers and suck them off. Fuck, I'm about to come. I need to eat her out, so I growl and slam her arms above her head. "Keep these here. I want to feast on your pretty slit. I want you coming before I tear apart your pussy."

"Are you sure?"

"Don't ever ask that again. If I want your pussy, all you need to do is serve it to me. Understood?"

"Yes."

"Good girl." I kiss her roughly and then pull back. "Keep those arms up there. I'm already too close to coming, and I want to come buried deep inside you."

The first swipe of my tongue nearly sends her off the bed again, so I press my forearm over her hips, holding her down while my other hand allows my fingers to play her pussy like a piano. I'm hitting the right notes, and my woman comes as I lave her clit. Her voice cracks as she screams my name. I have to reach down and squeeze my cock to stop me from nutting on the bed.

I push down my pajama pants, grateful that I'd forgone the boxer briefs, and line my cock up with her entrance. Heated, I push forward. At first, I send the first two inches in, but then she cries out and I freeze. "Just relax." She takes a calming breath, and I send the rest of me forward.

"Oh my goodness." The next gasp is much harsher. "It's so big. I feel so full."

"Relax, sweetheart." I rub her pussy, strumming her nub, trying to calm her down, but I'm so much larger than I guess a virgin should have. Maybe I need to have a talk with my father. Then again, maybe not. I sure as fuck can't talk to my godfather.

"I'm sorry, baby. Do you want me to stop?" In my mind, I'm silently pleading for her not to tell me to stop.

"No, let's just go slow." I nod and gently kiss her lips. We kiss over and over until I can feel the tension slip from her body. My fingers tease her nipples that are hardened from my touch. She feels so good, even though she's squeezing the life out of me.

I need to move, but I know I can't hurt her any more than I have. Slowly I test my movements, and she doesn't flinch, so I go a little further, pulling out a little more before sliding in again, each stroke moving a little more quickly. I move into a better rhythm, and it feels as though she's with me.

"Miles, it feels so much better now."

"That's good, baby girl, because it feels really good to me, and I hate that I was hurting you."

"Well, I had no idea you were carrying a dang flag pole in there."

"Thanks, Princess." I rock forward, working her pussy with my cock and fingers because I promised that I'd make her come, and I'm not a fucking chump. "Now be a good girl and come for me." I lean down and suck her nipple into my mouth and set her off. She cries out, coming with my name on her lips.

I lose control and pump my load hard and deep inside her. Elsa is in more trouble than she thought because my obsession with money and power aren't even close to the top anymore. Hearing her call out my name becomes my new addiction.

CHAPTER EIGHT

ELSA

IT'S BEEN AN INCREDIBLE FIRST WEEK TOGETHER. NIGHT AFTER night, we come home and make passionate love to each other after a hard day's work. My body aches from orgasm after orgasm, but I can't get enough. It's become an addiction. Some would think I'm crazy, maybe even need medication, but there is no way I'll fight this desire.

I enter the house after my last class, but I know that Miles will be at the hotel for another hour or two. He and my brother work so many hours, it's ridiculous. I'm glad they are teamed up together because it frees up their time, even though they are both insanely busy.

"Welcome home, Miss Elsa," Carl says, smiling a little to brightly for my tastes. Maybe I'm moody because I want to be greeted by my husband and not his employees. A part of me wanted to go to the hotel, but it's childish to bother him at work.

"Where's Mistress?" I ask, wondering why she didn't just scurry up to me like she always does.

"In the library," he states.

"Why?" Normally she's not allowed in there without one of us because there is a lot of things she can damage when she's unsupervised. I rush in there, and lying on the sofa with a book in hand is my darling fiancé and our puppy at his feet. They both perk up and look at me when I enter.

"I was wondering how long it would take for you to come home."

"Why didn't you tell me you'd be home early?"

He sets the book on the table next to the sofa and sits up. "I only arrived ten minutes ago, Princess."

"I didn't see your vehicle."

"It's in the garage. You sound suspicious. I came home early to see you, baby girl." He taps his lap and gives me that dark stare. "Come here."

"Oh." I bite down on the edge of my bottom lip, rubbing my inner thighs together.

"What's wrong?" he asks while his eyes move to the hem of my dress. His tongue peeks out from his mouth, sliding lazily over his lips.

"Nothing. I just missed you, and I was going to surprise you."

"Surprise me with what?" he asks, brows lifting in a lecherous way.

"This." I unzip my dress and then let it fall to the floor.

"Fuck, Elsa. Princess, I love this." I bought a new bra and panty set in Dallas with the girls, but I never had a reason to wear it because it was too provocative. Miles's admiring gaze makes it all worth the wait.

"Come here. It's time for you to show me what you have under these panties." He reaches out and slides his finger under the strap of my panties, rubbing my hip. "Climb up on the sofa."

"What?" I gasp and release a moan.

"You heard me, fiancée. Get that pussy up in my face."

"You want to eat me like this?"

"Yes, you threw down the damn gauntlet, woman, so bring that pretty kitty over here." I climb up onto the cushions with my heels on. I'm staring at him so that we're face to face.

He slides his fingers between my legs and strums my pussy over the lacy material, soaking the fabric. "That's right. You're a good girl, baby. Spread those legs. Tell me what you want. You wore this to tempt me, so tell me what you want me to do to your sexy body."

"I want you to eat me out like I'm a five-course meal."

"Damn right, sweetheart. I'm starving." My lips are crushed by his. "I'm going to eat you up, and then I'm going to ruin you all over again. This week has just been a sample of what our life will be like. I am not going to stop worshipping your naked body."

"Miles, please don't."

"Don't what?"

"Don't stop," I plead, tilting my head to the side, allowing Miles's tongue to dip along my collar bone. "Oh lord. You make me so wild," I confess.

The man is insanely talented, and he's making sure to give me what I need. His hand slips down the front of my body, snaking under the ruined panties. "Fuck, Princess. You're soaked."

"What are you going to do about it, Miles?"

"Use it to my advantage, of course." I'm quickly lifted up, and my pussy is riding his face. I don't even feel the panties falling off my body, but I see them in his hand as he caresses my arm. His mouth works at my core, dragging every damn drop of juice out of me. I cling to the back of the sofa, body rocking forward. Slowly I try to lift up and not suffocate him, but he growls, smacking my ass. "Ride me, baby."

"Fuck, I'm coming." My thighs shake around his head and I throw my body forward, trying to ride out the violent orgasm tearing through me.

"I need you in me now," I pant, feeling so damn heated. I don't know what dam he broke, but I want him—big dick, talented tongue, and all. I drop down to my knees and undo his belt. Mistress yelps and barks at us.

"Go lay down," Miles orders, and she does. "Mommy is fine."

"Better yet, stay put." He gets up off the sofa with his cock still tucked away, but his pants are undone and his face is glistening with my wetness. He opens the library door and calls for Mistress. "Go play, Mistress." She runs out the door. "Daddy has to thank Mommy for his present." He locks the door and turns to me.

"Now, where were we?" He smirks and then stalks toward me. "Turn around and bend over."

"You don't want me to suck—" He twirls his finger in a circular motion, telling me to spin around.

"Honey, if you suck my dick, I'll be nutting between those talented lips in seconds. Even though I can't get you pregnant yet, I want to feel my cum splash that tight pussy, coating it."

I get into position and pose with my ass out and head over the edge of the sofa. "Oh God, Miles. Please fuck me."

He comes up behind me and lifts my hips. I feel the thick length rub against my slit as he teases me. "Fuck, you're all wet. Someone's ready to take my big dick today."

"Yes, I am. I need it."

He grunts as he presses into me. I can feel my body shake with pleasure as he fills me up from behind. How can I be so close when I just came? Miles lays one hand on the middle of my back and the other rests on the back of the sofa. His face is right next to mine as he warns me, "Hold onto something, love. I'm about to test the strength of this furniture."

He pumps faster and faster, rocking the wood off the floor. "Yes, yes," I cry out, moaning. "Fuck me hard." He drives deeper into me, pressing my face into the back of the cushions.

"Can you come again?" He reaches under and strokes my mound, rubbing that perfect spot.

"Yes, I'm so close." It's not long until I'm squirting all over his hand and cock.

"Fuck, yes," he roars, filling me up. We collapse on the soft cushions.

"The sofa survived," I whisper, and then I hear a crack. "Well, mostly."

"It's okay. It will be fun to pick out a new one to ruin." He growls and attacks my throat and mouth with kisses as the sofa's feet continue to buckle. One gives out, and we bounce slightly as we angle a little toward the floor.

"I guess it's time to get dressed and head upstairs. You said you wanted pizza before you left for school, so we can order it before we jump in the shower."

"Love it."

"Good. Get moving before this sofa really gives out."

CHAPTER NINE

MILES

BACK TO BUSINESS AS USUAL, BUT THIS TIME I HAVE AN EXTRA pep in my step. "I know that fucking look, and I want to knock it off your face."

"Excuse me," I ask my future father-in-law. He's got a big attitude since Elsa and I became official.

"You're overly happy and my daughter didn't come by last night so I can only make the assumption that—"

I cut him off instantly. "If I were you, I'd stop yourself because whether it's me or anyone else, it was bound to happen. I'm not smiling because of that anyway. I'm just happy. I hadn't realized what finally having her as my fiancée would mean, but it's a whole different feeling. The rush of...I don't know...pleasure...excitement. It's hard to define the way it runs through me."

"This is still going to take some getting used to. I remember Blade wanting to run through me all those years ago. Hell, almost all the Riders did at one point." He chuckles to himself while he relives the memory.

"How is Milo with all of this? He and I haven't spoken about Elsa or at all since."

"Surprisingly, he's thrilled. I thought initially he was trying to keep you apart, but I realized he had mistaken the situation. When he comes back from his trip tomorrow, you should talk to him."

"I will." He left right after I snagged Elsa from their office, so I couldn't talk to him and explain that I'm madly in love with her. He's my closest friend and deserves the right to know that I'm obsessed with his baby sister.

"She needs to visit her mother, who misses her."

"I'm not stopping her. She was over like three times this week. I'm starting to think you're just upset about Elsa not being home." Yesterday they had a family dinner, but I took my beautiful woman out on a nice date which she deserved.

"You're right."

"I'm not taking her away. We live a short distance away, and we all run the same company. I love Elsa, and I'd never take her away from her family. Vegas is my home, and Elsa is my number one priority, and so is her happiness." I continue. "So what are we dealing with when it comes to our problems? Right now, no one is trying to make any moves. The announcement of our engagement went out, and I've heard from every family except the Santos family. You?"

"I heard from Santos. He told me I was foolish to allow a thug to be with my daughter. I explained that as your godfather, I knew exactly who you were, and I didn't know a better man."

"Thanks for lying for me."

"It's not a lie, but it doesn't change that I don't like you fucking my daughter."

"Daddy," Elsa gasps from the doorway.

"Elsa," he utters with a shocked look on his face.

"Damn. Where is my assistant?" he snarls. I hide my smug expression because he deserves the scolding even if Elsa doesn't learn to knock.

"He told me it was just the two of you in here, and I just barged in."

"Well, then, you will hear things you don't like," I say, walking up to my future wife. "What brings you here, love?"

She glares at me and then says, "I wanted to let you know that I have a study session tonight, so I'll be home late."

"I thought you weren't doing that anymore," my father says. Although she lives with me now, her parents are still involved with her life and I don't expect that to change too much. Despite his annoyance with me fucking his daughter, I love the man. We're all tight knit and as soon as we add to our little family, I'm sure they'll be invading our home for visits.

"I need a little extra help, and besides, Miles is busy until midnight," she reminds him. It annoys her when I work late, but there isn't much I can do about it.

"That's fine, but security will be a little heavier because it's late," I informed her.

"That's okay." She shrugs her shoulders without giving me any damn grief.

I press my lips on hers and whisper, "I love you."

"I love you too." She cradles my jaw, rubbing my stubble. She loves the way it feels, so I keep it short and neat. With a pat, she kisses my lips one more time.

"See you later, Daddy." She waves goodbye and then walks away. I stop her before she gets to the door when I remember something.

"Did you eat lunch?" I questioned, knowing she's forgetful when she's busy.

"Um...not yet, but I will."

"You better, or you'll get spanked." The warning comes with a growling kiss against her temple.

"I will. I promise." I kiss her again and then send her off.

I walk to the desk and call the front security desk where Kyros is. "Kyros, follow my woman and let me know if she eats. Also, watch that fucking TA of hers. Her other security patrol told me that he was staring at her a little too long."

"Yes, Sir." I end the call and look at my godfather as he chuckles.

"What?"

"Nothing. I wondered if you were going to let her get away with that shit."

"Nope. She dropped that study session for a reason, and my guy told me it was because that asshole was creepy. I'm trying to be understanding and not be overbearing. This is as far as I'll step back, but if he tries anything, he'll disappear."

"You're nicer than I am."

"It's not about him. It's about making her happy and trusting her choices."

"Damn, I don't know who taught you how to be such a good man." He starts adjusting his suit jacket.

"Whatever. Let's get to work because I'm sure your wife will be here to drag you away at five exactly." We work our asses off, closing contracts for the rest of the month as well as managing several problems around the casino and hotel. At five on the dot, Mrs. Martin comes and snags her husband because he is still limited on his work hours. She wants him at a hundred and isn't letting any one of us get away with shit.

It's around one in the morning when I get home and slide into bed beside my beautiful fiancée. She looks so peaceful, but I know she's hiding the truth from me. That bastard is still interested in her and is going to be a problem. I'll get her a tutor who can keep his or her eyes and hands to themselves. I tried not to interfere, but I won't tolerate someone lusting after her. Although he's not touching her physically, his desire is clear to every single one of my men. It won't be long until he tries something dumb and I have to kill the bastard.

"You're home," she whispers sleepily.

My lips brush her hair. "I'm sorry. I didn't mean to wake you."

"I missed you, Miles."

"You should have come to the hotel. We could have spent the night there if you wanted."

"Are you sure that's okay?"

"I have a suite available for me."

"No offense, but I don't want your special rooms."

"Baby girl, I thought I made myself clear that you're my only one."

"You said you had no mistresses, but you don't need mistresses for one-night stands or quickies."

"Well, I'm telling you now. You don't have to worry one bit. No doubt those rooms are for when I work too damn hard or I pull too many hours." I pull her into my arms so she's resting on my chest. "Look at me. Don't worry. I love you, and I don't want you to be upset."

"Are you too tired for me?" she asks.

I chuckle. "Never." I flip her onto her back and show her that she's my only one.

———

"Hey, Milo, it's been one damn long week since you've been on business. I'm starting to wonder if your ass was intentionally avoiding me."

"Ha-ha. Nah, brother. Not at all. I have acquired two more offers for the European hotels, but I need to go over them with both you and my father. I'm not making any moves without you two." He takes a seat in front of my desk. "So I'm guessing you want to talk about you and my sister, right?"

"Yeah."

"I hope you haven't fucked it up already because I'm going to have to kill you."

"Everything is wonderful. I'm just trying to see if we're cool," I say.

"As long as my sister is happy, I'm good."

"Seriously?"

"Yeah, I've never even seen you with a woman, so the fact that you want to marry my sister means you've learned a lot from our parents. Good luck, because she learned a lot too, which means she's used to being a princess."

"I know, and I'm prepared."

"Good. Now, how about we get out of here and speak to my dad about the deals, because I need some sleep?"

"Works for me." We head out of my office and walk down to my godfather's office. With that problem down, I'm feeling great about my relationship. All I have to do is keep an eye on the families. So far, they haven't made any moves, and it looks like they're not interested. At first, I thought there was about to be trouble, but maybe I overestimated their intentions.

I'm not letting this go, though. No, not until I'm certain that the threat is gone. Any sign of weakness on our part means that they'll strike. Several times over the years there have been attempts at hostile takeovers and knocks on the door by the Feds with RICO questions over the years.

Now they're trying to connect themselves by marriage; that isn't happening because she is mine—forever.

CHAPTER TEN

ELSA

"Have a good day, beautiful," Miles whispers against my throat as he slides up behind me. I don't think I'll ever get used to this rush that I've longed for since I was barely a teen.

Spinning around in his arms, I look up at him and love the fact that he didn't have time to shave this morning. I caress his scruffy jaw. "I'll try, but since someone made me so sore, I'm having a hard time walking."

He pulls me in so I can feel just why I ache. "You can always skip class."

"No, you know I can't," I huff, gently pushing away from him enough to get some distance from his dangerously tempting cock. He's not serious, but the lecherous look in his eyes tells me that he'd gladly play hooky with me.

He sighs and then smiles. "It's fine. I have to work anyway. Let me walk you out," he says, taking my book bag and slinging it over his shoulder. "Fuck, Princess. This thing is ridiculous. You shouldn't be carrying this."

"It's not that bad." I reach for it, but he stops me and takes my hand.

"I love your independence and strength, but while I'm around, it's not necessary."

"Are you always going to be like this?"

"Yes. I thought you would have gotten used to this, having grown up with your father."

"I did. I just don't want to be disappointed once the honeymoon phase ends."

"There is no honeymoon phase for us, Princess."

"I will see you tonight at home."

"That you will. We have a wedding to plan." He gently rubs my engagement ring that I love so much. I can't believe I was so damn blind to his love. What was wrong with me?

I squeeze his strong fingers that hold mine. "Yes, but I'm sure my mother would love to be involved in all of that, as would yours."

"The more, the merrier. As long as you're my wife, nothing else matters, Elsa." I arch up on my toes and kiss his lips before getting into my car. "Be careful."

"I always am." I smile and drive off. His parents are coming up next week to spend some time shopping for the wedding and talking plans. I love his mom. She's so talented, and I wonder if she'll be up to performing at our wedding. She's a professional pianist, and his parents met at one of her shows.

I smile when I think about how much love our parents have spread to us. Miles shows me every single moment. When I get to school, I get a message from him.

Stay safe, my love. I can't wait for tonight.

Me either. I love you more.

Not possible.

I don't even respond because I don't have time, and I'm not going to win. He'll probably show up here, carry me right out of class, and fuck me on the nearest isolated place. Smiling all morning, I make it through my first class and then run into my bestie.

"Girl, I love how happy you are." She hugs me so hard.

"Thanks. Can a girl be this happy? I am spoiled."

"Duh, but you deserve it. Now only if your hot brother would notice me, that would be great."

"I'll put in a good word for you." I wink.

"Please don't. I think I would die."

"Ange, you are ridiculous. Have you even given him the

slightest hint that you like him? You know they are clueless when it comes to things like that."

"I know, but I'm sure he doesn't like me, so it's cool. Anyway, we're going to be late. Can we catch up tomorrow and do a girls' day?"

"I'd like that."

"Awesome. I miss my bestie." We hug again before going our separate ways, and I head toward my next class. There's a sign on the front door saying to use the side entrance, so I swiftly turn around and then there's a large explosion near the area I just left with Ange. I look back to see what's happening and pray she's nowhere near there, but I'm stopped by a hand to my mouth. I bite at the hand, only to feel a pinch on the skin of my arm.

"Oh my God. Let me go." He drags me off as if I weigh nothing. Suddenly I can't move my body, as if I've lost control of it. What the hell happened to me, and where is my security? I heard the commotion in the quad, but I'd been almost to the main doors of the building to my next class when it happened.

"What are you doing? Where are you taking me?" The world around me spins, and everything moves at lightning speed.

"You'll see."

"Oh my God, it's you."

I haven't seen him since I ran away two years ago, but he looks so different. It's like he's done something to his face. "Yes it's me. I look a little different, don't I?" I don't say anything, but my silence is all he needs to continue. "You have your fucking filthy-ass brother to thank for that. I should give you what you deserve, but just looking at you makes me fucking sick."

He makes a gagging sound, then clears his throat. "I want to destroy your entire family. Killing you would accomplish that nicely, but I wouldn't get enough joy out of that. I want you to witness their deaths before you die." He tries to laugh maniacally, but it comes out weakly because his voice cracks. I don't know what the hell happened to him, but he clearly is messed up and he wants his revenge.

I close my eyes and pray that my family realizes that I'm missing. There was an incident at school when he grabbed me. What if my guards were harmed in the process?

"Don't go praying that someone is going to save you," he sneers, grabbing my face roughly before shoving me down on the cold floor. I'm not sure where he's taken me, but there's not a lot of light or exits in the room. The walls are made of stone, and the floor is cold. My heart's racing as I think about my trackers. My engagement ring is gone, and I know Miles had one in there for my safety and one for the ring in case it was lost. Still, my dad made sure I had several on me.

I'm in my clothes, but my shoes and bracelets are gone. The bastards are smarter than they look, but I have a chip in my thigh. All my father has to do is track it. Hopefully it still works and can track me.

"What does it matter if you're going to kill me anyway?" I'm not sure why I'm goading a madman.

"It doesn't, but I left a mess at the school. I'm not going to just make it easy for them to find you. Your dad, your mother, and your brothers will all pay for what they did to me. Just because you're a little fucking prude. You weren't that damn special. Just another dumb little spoiled princess and everyone thought you were protected by some rich thug. Ha." He shakes his head, smiling to himself like he has his own little private joke. "That's funny. He couldn't protect you from me because he's too busy. You're not that important to him, not even a bit. He's probably chasing some whore at his hotel. By the time they realize you're gone, they're not going to know where to find you."

"You're the sick one—so damn twisted. I can't believe you found me. I can't believe you're even here. I don't know what happened. I'm sorry for whatever they did, but this has nothing to do with me."

He tilts his head in a demented manner with his eyes turning cold and full of fury. "It has everything to do with you. This is all your fucking fault, you stupid bitch," he screams so violently that spit shoots from his crooked jaw. I swipe it away from my face.

"You're one of those guys who pretend to be one thing, but you're really not. I made the mistake of even thinking that you were nice."

"Wah, wah, wah, you are such a whiny little bitch.

Especially since you gave your pussy up to a man who is far from nice."

"I don't care what you have to say about Miles because it's a lie, and anything that you say or do from now on holds no weight with me. You're holding me captive, and you physically abused me, therefore nothing that comes out of your mouth has any value. My daddy always told me that a man that hits a woman isn't a man, so I don't care what you have to say about my family or my fiancé. Do your best because I've seen you, and you are the worst."

He grows angrier and then his fist comes down one more time. The room spins for a brief moment, and then I hear other voices. "Please be help," I whisper.

"No one is coming to help you." I recognize the voice from the hotel, but it isn't someone that worked for my father or Miles. He's one of the men who tried to buy my father out. He slams my head down and I pretend to black out, but I won't forget his face and voice.

CHAPTER ELEVEN

MILES

An alert hits my phone before it rings. It is Kyros. "There was an explosion at the campus quad. It was a small bomb in the garbage can. Only two injuries and both are our guys, but Elsa's missing."

"Fuck, it was planned. Are you tracking her?"

"Yes, but the signal drops about ten miles from the location. Her ring was probably dumped on the highway out of town." She has more trackers, but if they saw the ring, they probably pulled all her jewelry and her book bag. She has one in her tennis shoes, so if he's wise, he took them off too. God, the thought of him taking her clothes off sends me into a fit, and I punch the wall, breaking a large glass cabinet.

"Oh my god, Boss, is everything okay?"

"Get Emiliano in here now," I roar.

He rushes into the room, and I shout, "Someone's kidnapped Elsa."

The color fades from his face, and he barely makes it to my sofa. I'm afraid I nearly gave the man a heart attack. We call a medic and then get him care while I attempt to find out who took his precious daughter and the love of my life.

Fuck, I didn't mean to send him to the hospital. Within ten minutes I've made all the calls, and my men are back from the campus with a special guest.

They've gathered in the interrogation area of the casino where we question thieves or card counters. As soon as I arrive, my fist makes contact with the bastard. I already hated the fucker, but he's bumbling and not giving me the answers I need.

"Where is she?" I bark into the face of the stupid TA who has been fawning over my woman. I learn he has an eager interest in her beyond doing his job. I want to smash his head in, but I don't have time to deal with him.

"I don't know," the punk squeals. He's the man my security team mentioned was a little too friendly to her during class and often stopped her before she left for the day.

"You're lying. You've been watching my fiancée, so you better speak up before I cut off your tongue."

"I swear that I haven't seen her since she left this morning, but she wasn't alone."

"Who was she with?" I demand, grabbing his collar and staring at this weakling in the face.

"First, it was the girl Angie that she meets up with, but then they parted ways and she went to her next class, but it looked like the doors were closed so she went off to the side. I didn't see her go in because the explosion happened and I turned to see it. When I finally looked back, I thought she went to class just like they did." He points to Elsa's security who are bandaged. They were charred from the explosion yet are safe, whereas my woman is gone.

How the hell did she get taken? She'd been safe, protected, or so I thought. Johnny wasn't anywhere near her, and neither were any of the other families. If it wasn't those assholes, then who could have taken my future?

We have only been engaged for a week. We foolishly thought she was safer now that everyone knew she was engaged to me, but that only seemed to make her a greater target.

I love her with all my heart and soul, and if anything happens to her, there will be no end to what I won't do to seek my revenge. The thought of losing her is unbearable.

"Get this little bitch out of here. If I see him ever again, I'm going to put a bullet in his head and dispose of his body in the desert." They drag his ass out and I return to my office to look for answers, but what I need is a way to find her.

I'm waiting for news from campus, and it's been over an hour. Kyros went there to get information from the school. If I have to hack the system, I will. In fact, I'm loading my system right now. I don't have time for permission. I get a text from him.

KYROS

I'm in. They don't want problems from one of their prominent citizens.

ME

Good. I need answers now.

I pace my office, pouring myself a drink. The sting on my hand doesn't even bother me anymore, but it's nothing because I'm going to do so much worse later when I go on a rampage. So far I haven't heard from anyone about a ransom, which scares the fuck out of me.

My godfather enters, and I remark, "I thought you'd be in the hospital."

He chuckles like a madman. "You are fucking crazy if you think I'd let the devil take me before I find my baby girl."

"Good. I need all the help I can get because I'm about to burn the world to the ground for her." I'm doing my best to maintain control.

"They gave me an adrenaline shot and a warning to rest, but I don't give a fuck."

"I've contacted the families, and so far, they all claim she wasn't taken by their men. Novak offered his services, but I turned them down. I'm not owing anyone unless we need them."

"We don't. We have our own people. The only way they'd know more is if they're involved," Milo snarls, entering behind him and fixing his suit. I don't miss the .357 on his person. He's ready for war, which is good because it's time.

"If any of them are involved, they will pay until there is nothing left. I don't care if she even just chipped a damn nail."

"I've got a lead. Someone nabbed her from her class after she met with Angie, her friend." I shake my head because I'm so damn furious at how I failed her and how her guards had failed their tasks, but knowing that there had been an intentional diversion to distract them while she was still twenty feet from their reach had pissed me off even more. If we had her on a tight leash like we preferred, her guards wouldn't have given her an ounce of space.

My main line rings, and I answer it. "Ivanov."

"It's Santos. I wanted to say I'm sorry about your fiancée. I wanted to let you know that my son and I have nothing to do with her disappearance."

"Why are you calling me?"

"Because Johnny's on his way there. I told him to mind his damn business, but he's bringing Miss Stevens, who has information for you. I want you to leave him be because he's only doing this to protect her."

"Fair enough." I know he's not involved, but it's interesting that he is bringing her along. "As long as he doesn't start shit, everything will be fine. All I want is my woman back."

A moment later, my office door slams open. "What's the news on her?" My father storms through the door with three other Riders I didn't expect to see: Boomer, Blade, and Wrench. They got here fast as fuck, which took me by surprise. I check the clock, and it has been less than four hours since I called my father.

"You got here fast as fuck."

"We took the fast jet, and we might have broken some FAA laws."

"We need to find my niece now," Blade snaps, grinding his knuckles. He grips my godfather's shoulder. "How is my sister?"

"Barely hanging on."

"Damn it. We need to find Elsa," he snarls.

"Miss Angela is here to see you, Miles," my assistant says from the wide-open doorway.

"Bring her in here." She scurries in, looking a mess. Her face is tearstained, and her arm is bandaged. Johnny Santos isn't anywhere to be found.

"What happened to you?"

"I was knocked down in the chaos. It was like a stampede near the can. I'd just dumped my cup about ten seconds before the explosion, so I was pretty close. Anyway, none of that matters. I only found out about Elsa when Johnny said his dad asked if he'd messed with her again."

"Where the fuck is Johnny now? What do you know?" I ask.

"He left because he said I was safe with you all, but to call him if I needed anything."

"You don't need to call him for shit," Milo snarls.

She looks up and him angrily and then directs her attention to me. "I think I know who took her. It was the guy from prom. I didn't realize it at first, until I learned she was missing. It took me a minute, but I saw him on campus today, so it had to be him."

"Do you mean Jacob?" Milo says.

"Yes. I swear it was him, except he looked a little different."

My phone rings, and it's my team leader at the scene so I raise my hand to stop the conversation. "Security here has footage, and I'm sending it to you now to do your thing with the software." He explains the info, and I get to my computer, waiting for the footage while I boot my tracking system.

"He's caught leaving the campus in an ambulance. We've traced it. We've sent a team to search for it, but I'm not sure if they changed vehicles."

"Keep on it." I look back at everyone after I end the call.

"Angie, thank you. Please go home and get some rest. Someone will escort you there."

"Please let me know when you bring her home safe. We were supposed to have a girls' day tomorrow." She wipes tears from her face. It's the first time I'm hearing this, but I know Elsa said she'd been neglecting her bestie and they needed to hang out again. Maybe they just made plans.

"Hopefully soon," I add.

As soon as she's gone, Emiliano looks right at his son and asks, "What the fuck happened, Milo?"

He drops to one of the chairs, running his hand over his face. "The night of prom, the bastard drugged her and attempt to assault her, but she ran to the bathroom and called Mom."

"That was over two fucking years ago." His chest is heaving with anger.

"Take a fucking seat before you pass out." The man nearly died earlier today and he's pushing it.

"Who the fuck was going to tell me about this?" he barks out.

"I thought I'd handled it, Dad."

"Your mom didn't tell me either." There was a sense of betrayal in his tone that I knew hurt.

Milo sighed. "It's not like mom didn't want to tell you, but Elsa asked us not to. She was mortified and afraid that you've never let her out of your sight again."

"Damn fucking right."

"Security was high on her. She already wasn't leaving the house after this happened." He scrunched his brows together like he was remembering something.

"So why didn't you kill him?"

"The only reason I didn't kill the bastard was because there were too many people that knew she was the last one with him."

"What did you do to him?" I ask, wanting all the details.

"I permanently disfigured the son of a bitch and sent him on his way without the ability to hurt a woman again. I told him if I ever caught him in town that I'd kill him. I thought he learned his lesson. I had no idea he was going to come back to get her."

"He's a fucking fool," Boomer adds. "Does he have any idea who he's fucking with?"

"This time, I'm going to end him."

I shake my head because the privilege will be mine. "No, I'm going to do it. He touched my fucking woman."

"I don't care; I'm going to be the one to kill him."

His father steps between us and snarls, "First come, first serve. I don't care who does it. He doesn't walk away. Understood?"

"Understood," we answer simultaneously.

I check my messages, and the ambulance was dumped along with all her things. Damn it. It only gives us a small lead. "It looks like all our trackers are lost unless she has one we don't know about."

My dad pulls out an older model phone and smirks. "Get ready for war, boys. All her trackers were disposed of, save one. The signal is faint, so we have to get moving just in case they move."

My godfather smirks and then says, "I'm sure it's the one that I had put in her hip when she was thirteen." I look at her father like he's twisted, but I also want to hug him.

"In her hip?"

"Yes, it was a crazy idea, but I thought it was for the best."

"It took me forever to get the damn system to run."

"Thanks, Cyber."

"You should have told me."

"It was Cyber who remembered because he had similar devices on your mother. I fucking forgot about it. I don't know if you noticed that I had a damn heart attack when you told me someone took my daughter."

"Where is she?" I asked my father.

"In the fucking woods."

We all move like our asses are on fire. Nothing can stop me from getting to my woman. Luckily we were already prepared to go so my men had the vehicles set. "We need to get moving because it's about forty miles from here and I want all of them dead."

"You don't believe they killed her, do you?" Milo asks as we hit the road.

"You better pray they haven't," I say to Milo. I mean that with my whole heart. No one will come out alive today, and I will bury every single body that laid a hand on my precious Elsa.

"I'll kill myself," he mutters. I think to myself that he won't have to.

"Let's go. We need an arsenal." We take three large SUVs while I have my men already in the vicinity looking for her. They won't approach without my orders. If something happens to my Elsa because they fucked up, I'll enjoy every minute of slow torture I give them.

"We brought one," Boomer says with a grin. Blade pulls out his favorite knife, and I can't shake the violent pleasure I'm feeling. I want to rip apart everyone involved. It will be fun.

"Thank you." I knew we could count on them. They were always ready for war and we need the best. My men are good, but nothing like the Riders. I heard so many stories through my childhood, including the one about my mother's attack and I never thought I'd have the same problem. I'm grateful to have them at my side.

We're nearly on top of the beacon, so we keep our distance and unload what we need for a ground and aerial assault. My heart pounds in my chest as I consider what he's probably doing to her. I close my eyes and pray she has the strength to hold out until I get there.

The house is in the middle of nowhere. It appears to be a small shack made of wood, but it's clearly not. Underneath, it's a layer of steel. My father's tools are brought out to scan the area for bombs and traps. Any metal and surveillance are the first things we pick up on. We're just two klicks away from the location. There are ten men surrounding the cabin, letting us know she's alive. If she wasn't, there would be no need for security.

I send up a silent thank you for that, but now it's time to get her out safely.

My father pulls me in for a one-armed hug. "We will get her back, and then we will destroy them all."

"There is a surveillance system, but I can dummy it up and it won't trace us. It's not a heat sensing one. It's probably because of the wildlife. They were either too cheap or annoyed by the constant animals in the area. Either way, it's not up. They do have four sensors on the perimeter to go off if anyone crosses this area, but I've already turned them off. They are simpletons. Now, fellas, it's time to go old school."

"Boys, we taught you how to fight and how to kill. Don't lose your nerve, or you will be the one to die."

"Yes, Uncle," Miles tells Blade. He taught us how to use every weapon with precision.

"Here you go." He hands me a special blade. "For your future wife, exact the revenge you deserve." He pats my back. It means the world to me that I have their respect and assistance. I know they're doing because she's their family, but also because I'm right for her.

"Thanks."

"Listen up, I have a plan," Blade says. He breaks it down step by step and we all agree even if Milo isn't happy that he's left with little chance of confronting the bastard before I do. He had his chance and failed.

We stealthily move along the wooden path with the least number of leaves. Blade and I take the high ground, going from the trees with a zip line while the rest move along the forest floor.

With our blades out, we strike at the two guards on the roof, knocking them to the ground below. They're dead instantly. My father and hers are on the next two. We gently land on the roof and make our way to the hatch, entering with our guns ready. There are two rooms, and we're immediately confronted by two armed bastards. Startled, they can't pick up their weapons fast enough. I smirk as I let my rage loose. We end them and move on.

Outside, I know the others are getting the job done. The sound of their screams bring pleasure to my ears. I want them all to shout, but it's nothing until I find her. I want to tear everyone apart.

The place is small, but there are multiple doorways, Blade goes in one direction, while I take the other. I call out for her and hear nothing. She has to be close. Then I realize that there's another door, and I open it to see that it leads to a cellar. I rush down and find two men at the door.

I throw my knife and hit one in the chest. The other doesn't realize I have a gun, and he fires at me, but I duck out of the way. Once he stops to reload, I turn into the room and blast his ass. He's laid out, and then that's when I spot the fucking bastard Milo made. "Wow, no wonder you want revenge. That face and no dick either?" A light scoffing chuckle leaves with my insult.

"You piece of shit," he roars, but the damage has made him less scary. He rushes at me and tries to fight me, but he's no match. His swing is wide as we move around the room, and the door is open. We go at it in the stairwell.

I shove him back and he falls, busting his head against the edge of the stairs, cracking his skull open like a damn egg. "Well, motherfucker, that was anticlimactic." I walk down and look for my woman.

There she is in the middle of the room, looking petrified— *of me.*

CHAPTER TWELVE

ELSA

HIS BODY IS HEAVING AS HE STARES AT ME WITH ALL THE carnage around the room red and bloody as Jacob bleeds out. My body is in the center of the room, curled up. I'm afraid, but not of him, at least not that he'd hurt me. I'm never worried that he would hurt me, but what if he hates me? Slowly his eyes soften, and his steps move evenly toward me. "Miles," I mutter. "I... I..." I continue to stammer, but the words are unable to form.

Before I'm able to utter another syllable, his men follow behind him.

"Leave us," he roars as his eyes stay focused on mine.

"Yes, Boss. Just wanted to let you know the house is clear and the family is waiting."

"Good." He crosses toward me. "Are you okay?" he asks me gently, as if he's afraid of my answer. "Did they hurt you?" He doesn't touch me for his own good or mine, but I need him.

"No more than you can see." He swallows hard.

"That I can see? Baby, you have bruises on you. I should kill him again." A tear slides down my face. He reaches out and wipes the wetness away. I lean into it, and he pulls me close.

"Miles, it's okay. They'll heal," I whispered, trying to sound strong as I lay my face on his chest. His lips brush the top of my head and then I move to look at him again.

"They shouldn't have been there in the first place, Elsa. You're my princess, and they put their hands on your precious skin." He raises my hand and then kisses my pulse. "No one should ever lay a hand on you." Slowly he caresses my jaw and then my temple, each one sending a shiver through my body.

Our mouths hungrily meet in a soul devouring kiss. I cling to him, forgetting everything but the feel of his strength as he holds me in his arms.

"Oh, Miles, don't stop," I plead. My voice is filled with a need that is so deep and uncontrollable. I feel his hardness press against my heat; even in this situation, I'm equally aroused. "This probably isn't the best time to have sex."

He lets out a small chuckle. "No, our dads and others are outside."

"But you're so hard," I whimper, grinding against him, trying to fight the sudden need for relief.

"Maybe I'm just so glad you're in my arms right now. I was worried I'd never see you again. I'd destroy the world like they destroyed mine."

I can't control the sobs that leave my voice, and I'm choking on them.

"I love you so much," he whispers against my ear. He pulls away and takes my hand, giving me some breathing room and that's when reality comes back in full force.

The scene before me is stark and frightening. Jacob's body is near the exit, and we can't leave without passing it. The smell of iron wafts through the air, pungent and foul. I can't handle it, and I nearly vomit in my mouth, but I contain myself.

"Can we go home?" I asked, wanting to get away from this awful place.

"Without a doubt. I just need to lie down in our bed and hold you to know you're safe." He scoops me up in his arms and carries me. "I can walk, Miles."

"Yes, and I saw the way you looked at the exit. I won't let you be upset again if I can help it." I loved this man more than he could ever know.

"Thank you."

We move toward the stairs where the piece of crap lies, and he kicks him in the balls.

My heart stammers and I panic, quickly clearing any doubts Miles might have. "He didn't touch me like that, if you're worried."

We stop, and he stares deep into my eyes. "Look at me, Elsa. I'm sorry, love. I would be worried that he violated you, but not for my sake. It would be for your sake. I would never want you to deal with that pain and horror. No woman should ever have to suffer such violation. However, I know he didn't."

"How did you know?" I asked, wondering how he could be so certain.

"Because he couldn't. Maybe that's why he wanted revenge so badly that he came back and was willing to risk everything. Your brother castrated him."

I slapped my hand to my mouth so fast it hurt. "Oh my God."

"Milo didn't want him to live and then go on to rape other women." I nod and press my head onto Miles's chest. There are no words for my brother's actions. I can't say he's wrong, but they led to today, so right now I can't rationalize it. The pain of it all is too real.

"Princess," my father sighs with relief when he sees me. There's blood on his face, and I know that he had to do things to get it there. He reaches for me, but Miles refuses to let me go.

"Miles, I'm okay." He sets me down and I go to my father who quickly throws his arms around me and squeezes me tightly.

"Baby, we thought we lost you." I sob against him as his body shakes with his own unshed emotions. "God, your mother has been devastated."

"Call her and let her know we have her," Miles states.

"We will once we are in a clear zone." We need to get moving. "We can't let anyone trace us here. The clean-up crew will be here to dispatch these assholes," Uncle Blade says.

"There had to be someone with power helping him. There was no way he was working alone. The guy was barely an adult," my father says.

"I recognized one of the guys," I add. Everyone turns to me with wide eyes.

"Who was it, baby?" Miles asks me, rubbing my back.

"I don't remember his name, but he was at the hotel one time when I was there."

"Does he work for us?" My father asks through clenched teeth. I could see the anger rolling off him, but thankfully the man didn't work for us. At least that man didn't.

"No, he was visiting you, and you two didn't agree. He gave me strange vibes and eyed me like a creep."

"Was he a Santos?"

"No. I know Mr. Santos from his son." Miles growls next to me. He drags me to his side, taking me from my father as if he has to maintain possession of me. I can't say I complain.

"Whatever, Miles. I went to school with Johnny so I've seen his father for years, but now that I think about it, this guy was at the school functions once or twice over the years."

"Let me know if you recognize any of these guys."

"I heard his voice too," I add. I close my eyes and let the memory return. "He told me no one was going to come help me."

"Sweetie, look at this and let me know if it's one of these assholes." My father hands me his phone, and I see a photo with a group of men that were sitting around Miles' dining room table. My eyebrows raise, and then I look at him as if he betrayed me.

"We had a meeting where I warned them to stay away from you."

"When was this?" I need to know when these people were in my new home.

"Before I went into surgery. Any sign of weakness to these men makes them want to strike at me." That's when Miles became like a second skin, always around, stalking me. Was he really just playing as a love interest to keep them at bay? "Sweetie, you were their interest, so I had Miles warn them off." There's a lump in my throat. My heart doesn't believe it. Still. I have to be sure.

"Is that why?" He presses a hand to my mouth.

Swiftly, I find my body flush to his with his gaze fixed on mine. "No, baby, don't do that. You know it's not true. The second they mentioned you, I nearly jumped over the table to clock them, giving away my feelings, and I knew damn well I was risking a lot." I nod, feeling his growing desire against my body again.

My uncle coughs beside us. "Um…any of them look like the guy?"

Miles releases me, and I look at the image again. "Yes, it's him."

"The bastard was wrong because we were always coming for you. Now he's going to pay," Milo says.

They shake their heads. "I can't believe Novak thought he was slick," my father says.

"The fool should have kept his mouth shut, and we wouldn't have been onto him so quickly. Now, it's time to get his ass." Miles clamps his lips shut as he seethes with rage.

Minutes later the vehicles pull up and it's Miles security with five SUVs. "Time go home," Miles says. We load up, and I sit beside my fiancé. They are making plans as I rest my head on Miles's chest, but I listen in.

"We're going fly you and your mother out to the Steeleville compound, and then you're staying put until we deal with our problem." Honestly, that sounds great. As tough as I am, I've had enough.

I jolt up and ask, "What about Mistress?"

"Mistress?" Wrench asks.

"Our dog," I answer.

"She's coming with. Don't worry, Princess. I wouldn't leave our baby without her mama." Miles kisses my forehead. "Now, we need to get moving before we draw any attention." The vehicles finally started moving and the first crunch of the leaves drew my attention to where I was kept prisoner.

We move fast past the small metal shack into the middle of the woods. When I look back, I can't believe he'd taken me so far away from home. I stare at the ground all around me. My body could have been lost to the earth below me. I would be part of the foliage, permanently buried if they didn't find me. I don't grasp that I'm crying until my face is wet. "Princess, what is it?"

"The reality...I just..." Miles tightens his arms around me, and the warmth takes away the sadness. I need him, but I understand that he needs to protect me and our future which means he has business to deal with. I sigh and close my eyes, resting on him again.

"Rest. We can talk about it when you're ready, but know this. We wouldn't have given up, Elsa. None of us." He kisses my temple and my soul doesn't ache as painfully as it did a moment ago.

"He's right," Boomer adds. "Not a one of us. Riders to the end, little girl." With their words of reassurance, I relax just enough to stop crying, but I can't sleep and I'm grateful for it because I can see how far he took me. We ended up forty miles from home.

As we pull into my parents' home, my family is waiting for me. Even though I see my brothers, it's the one person who I've always gone to comfort that I search for. My mother, whose eyes are red-rimmed and face blotchy, throws her arms around me.

"My baby," she sobs. Those tears break me and make me whole all at the same time.

"Mommy," I cry, needing her so much.

"I'm here. I'm here." We walk inside together, and she takes me over to the sofa where we sit down and she cradles my upper body like a little girl all over again. "Elsa, I almost lost you."

I sob harder and press my head into her chest. I need this.

CHAPTER THIRTEEN

MILES

SCORCHED EARTH.

That's what the fuck is going to happen. Watching my future wife throw herself into her mother's arms as her heart breaks is devastating. I understand more than I care to admit. When my mom called earlier, I felt her warmth, and I needed her comfort. She gave me that added strength to handle this crisis. She's always been the quiet solace for all of us.

"We'll be back. Don't let anyone in. If anyone comes here that is not on the approved list, be ready to end them," I warn the security. "No failure will be tolerated."

"Yes, Mr. Ivanov." I know it's Emiliano's house, but it's my woman, and I just killed for her. I plan to do a lot more for her.

There was a war about to take place, and I won't lose.

We have twenty men available and could have another twenty ready within hours, but it wouldn't be enough if Novak activated his street thugs. In order to coordinate, we head to my home where I have access to my advanced computer systems. My father and I can do a lot while Kyros and his team of men can track down his lackeys and keep tabs on his crew.

"We need to do this financially, Miles, and you know it." I pressed my lips together.

"Yes, Father. It seems history repeats itself. I need to dispose of my enemy in more than one way." He and I head to work with our computers, logging in with untraceable software and the latest malware and work to hack into Novak's systems.

The man is a dinosaur. He's only about ten years older than my father, but he acts like he's in his eighties. All his security files are running on old-school McAfee. I was hacking that before I was potty trained. It's like he's not even trying. I wonder if he's still running Windows 10. I try not to laugh at the old tech. It's no wonder we were able to get to the cabin so easily.

He's smart about some of the tech because it keeps me from hacking his cameras, but I have drones for that. My small stealthy bird drones are out on his property. Uncle Boomer loves that tech. It has become his favorite toy I've created. It's one of my hobbies.

Within hours, we know where everyone in his family is and where the old bastard is located. He thought he could run after learning my fiancée was safe. Tomorrow his credit cards won't work, then his belongings will be repossessed—day by day, he will lose everything. Only when he's at his lowest will I put my blade through his heart while I stare him in the eyes and let him know why.

I return to my in-laws with Kyros, and take my beautiful woman by the hand. "Are you ready to go home?"

She tilts her head and her pretty lips part. "I thought you said we are going to Steeleville."

"We are, but we need to pack, and I need some time alone with you. Does that bother you?"

"No, of course not, Miles." She turns her killer sunshine smile on me, making my heart quicken and my length grow.

"Good, I just need to hold you." We leave her family for the time being. I need her all to myself. Kyros holds the door open to my vehicle and drives us back so I have a chance to cradle my wife. "I love you so much, Elsa. I need you to know that. I'd never do anything to hurt you."

"I know that." I rub her cheek, hating that she has purple bruise on her soft skin. I'm so damn pissed that I want to bring Brodsky back to life and kill him again. She flinches and that hurts.

"I don't want you to ever be afraid of me."

She takes my hand and places it back on her face. "I'm not. I swear, Miles. You're my peace." I close my eyes and press my forehead to hers. "Honestly, I was worried about the touching thing, but I'm not anymore." I fiercely kiss her lips, but then I remember the bruising. It doesn't seem to bother her as much as before, but now that the adrenaline's worn off, it's a little rough.

She groans, so I back off. "I'm sorry, love."

"I'm not. I need your kisses. The pain only reminds me that I'm alive."

"I've got something else to show you how alive you are," I growl. She giggles when I lift her onto my lap, letting her feel my stiffness.

"Please. I need you, Miles." As soon as we get inside, I take her to our room where we shower off the day and make slow, passionate love. The way I devour every inch of her, she should have no doubts left about my love or desire.

By morning, we move our entire family down to Steeleville where they will be completely safe.

THE NEXT WEEK HAD BEEN NOTHING BUT PLANNING FOR OUR wedding while the Vegas world learned that Novak suddenly took his own life.

It's the strangest thing. Reports believe it's because he was going bankrupt, but others believe it was because he was diagnosed with an uncurable cancer and wanted to take the easy out. No one questioned his death when the news was so abysmal, and he'd lost so much money online gambling. Who knew the man had an addiction to sports betting that went back a decade? I did, since I made it up with actual receipts. It's amazing what you can do when you use your gifts for revenge.

Of course, I also planted the fake cancer report for good measure.

In reality, it's quite a different story.

Four days ago…

"It's good of you to see me," I say, entering his property unannounced and unseen. "Don't bother hitting that button. It doesn't work." I can see his hand under the desk where his emergency switch is located. It's really entertaining to see the color drain from a man's face when he realizes that he's face-to-face with the man he betrayed.

"What do you want?" he stammers.

"You tried to kill my woman." I remain calm and collected when I want to snap his neck.

He throws up his hands and shakes his head. "I didn't do anything. It was all Jacob Brodsky," he exclaimed, trying to save himself, but nothing could do that now.

"Yes, who happens to be your illegitimate child."

"How did you come to that realization?" After Elsa said she'd seen Novak at school, I wondered why he was there on occasion, I checked the student roster. His son graduated three years before Elsa did, so it didn't take long before I found out which kid he went to see.

"I've got the right people, and besides, after looking at that fucker, it was obvious he has your fucking crooked-ass nose. To think I assumed it was broken in a fight. You're just one ugly son of a bitch."

"Yeah, you sent him after her all those years ago, and now he's paid the price." From the look in his cold, beady eyes, he couldn't deny it if he tried. "Did you think we wouldn't find out?"

Forgoing the denials, he shrugs and says, "It took you so long to figure out he was related."

"We didn't know anything about the little shit and his attack on Elsa. She wanted the memory to be washed away. See, some women don't want to deal with the gross feeling that they were almost violated by someone they trusted. She was fortunate that he hadn't gotten to what he planned, but it was because she was trained and not isolated."

He slammed his fist down. "She wasn't even raped. She threw a fit, and my son paid for it."

"Really? He touched her, put his mouth on her, and he nearly got what he wanted, but she escaped his grasp. Seconds more, and he would have been buried years ago."

"Now, let's have a drink together before I finish what you started."

I pour a drink for each of us with the laced bottle and hand it to him. Of course, my people brought it in to match the one he had. It was his favorite and he was an avid drinker, so he quickly downed the first glass. "Damn. Save some for the rest of us."

"If you're going to kill me, I might as well get wasted first." He swirls his glass and grunts his disgust.

"I'm not going to kill you...yet."

He takes another large gulp down. I hide my smirk as I noticed the slow shake of his hand. This time, the drugs are affecting him.

"What did you do to me?" he asked as his body weakens.

"Nothing. You should see these." I set out his bank records and then his medical records.

"What the fuck?"

"See I don't need to kill you, Novak. You're already on the way out the door, and you're broke as fuck. Soon, you'll have nothing, and you're rotting from the inside out, which I could have told you without the tests."

"You bastard. Did you come here to gloat?" he asks.

"Duh. What the fuck did you think? I don't even have to lay a finger on you, even though I know you laid your hands on my woman. You struck her, and I could suffocate your fucking ass right now and no one would know." Although I'm not exactly telling the whole truth, it's fun to watch him. Slowly, he loses it. His breathing becomes shallow as the meds work overtime.

"You're a bastard."

"I can take these back."

"No, these are mine. I don't even know how you got access to them." Seriously, did this man know nothing about me? He might have gotten tests done, but the results were accidentally switched at the hospital.

Anyway, he tugged at his tie and then poured himself another glass and drank it as if to quench the thirst. He falls back on the chair, and I watch as he slowly dies. With precision, I switch the bottles, making sure to slide it into his hands, getting those necessary fingerprints. Then I pull out the prescription bottle of pills and add his fingerprints to those too, spreading out the necessary amount. I know how many were used and how many should roughly be in his system.

I snuck out the same way I came in and disposed of my fake print gloves. Using only back roads and my fellow Riders, I returned to Steeleville and my family.

It's been a wonderful vacation.

EPILOGUE

MILES

TWO YEARS LATER

THAT'S MY HOT WIFE IN HER ONE-PIECE SUIT. DAMN THEY could make a show about her sexy ass. No, no they couldn't because I'd kill motherfuckers for drooling over her. She leans over the body in the middle of a crime scene two miles off the strip. I just flew back from a trip to Steeleville while she was working only to find her on the scene of a murder case in the desert. Her long hair tied up in a bun, the warm dry air, blowing a few strands around and away from her lovely face.

She's bagging some evidence as I stand at the edge of the crime scene tape. I take out my phone and snap photos.

"Sir, may I ask why are you taking photos?" An officer asks. "This is a crime scene."

"That beautiful woman is my wife and frankly, I've never seen her in action. She's breathtaking even picking up potential evidence."

"She is." I let out a growl.

"What did you say?"

"I mean…"

"You mean that she is my wife and that if you want to not be the next dead body she examines that you keep your motherfucking eyes, hands, and mouth to yourself, correct?"

"Correct."

"Oh, Mr. Ivanov, it's good to see you," Chief of Police Aguirre says. She approaches with a smile. "I was just about to call you. We could use your expertise. I found a smashed drive that looks like it's been in the desert for more than a day. Maybe you or your specialized equipment could work your magic."

"Send it over and I'll see what I can do," I say with smirk. That's when my hardworking wife looks our way. I see her face harden and immediately I sense a hint of jealousy.

She stands, handing over the sealed bag to her assistant. Then she turns our way, and I wait expectantly for her arrival. "Mr. Ivanov," she says as she reaches us.

"Come on now. Elsa, you don't have to be so formal. We know he's your husband."

"I like to be professional."

The chief nods and then says, "Thank you, Mr. Ivanov. Our offices will be in contact."

I nod and return my attention to my wife who is full of questions, but they can wait. Her face is flush and beads of sweat run down the sides of her face. "Dearest love, do you need some water? It's a bit hot and I'd hate for the sun to get to you."

"I'm fine," she insists, but she's clearly upset.

"What time will you be done?"

"We are working until the scene is cleared and the evidence is logged and processed. I'm scheduled until eight, but it depends on how long things take."

"I'll be waiting." I wink and then add, "You look fetching, my wife." She blushes and then walks back to her work. I glare at the little twerp who had made the comment about my wife. He'll be reassigned tomorrow. I'll make sure of it.

The moment she steps through the door, I scoop her up in my arms. "Shower time."

"Put me down," she squeals as I rush her up to our bedroom. "I showered at work." I growl, angry at the idea of her showering around strangers.

Kicking our bedroom door closed, I dropped her onto the bed. "You were naked around other men." She lands on her back, but I'm quick to flip her onto her belly and pin her down.

"Are you nuts? Of course not. We have a women's locker

room. I didn't want to come home with any of the gunk on me."

"Gunk?" she nods fast.

"Well, I'm going to make you a dirty little mess and you'll need another wash up, Mrs. Ivanov," I whisper against her ear. I reach between the mattress and her, sliding my fingers under her cute pink leggings. Her firm ass is pressed nicely against my crotch. Damn, my pretty wife always looks so sexy in anything she wears, but she went to work in damn near hot pink leggings today, trying to drive motherfuckers wild.

"What are you doing in these dick teasing pants, wife?"

"Trying to tease my big dick husband because he came to my work looking hot."

"No need to be jealous, Princess. You know this big cock is only for you."

"Take off your top before I rip it to shreds." She does and I flick the clasp to her bra, letting it fall off. Next those brain draining pants have to go, so I yank down her leggings and slid them down her thighs. They reveal her pink thong panties and round cheeks. "Fuck, Elsa, you're asking for a thoroughly hard fucking today, aren't you?"

"Yes, I am." She pushes her ass back until it hits my hand.

"I love that you're asking for your spanking." My hand comes down on her bottom several times, turning it almost as bright as her panties. Elsa lets out a yelping cry each time I make contact with her supple flesh, and those sounds stiffen my already hard cock. My zipper digs into the bottom of my shaft. I reach down and adjust before freeing myself. The tip is already wet with a pearly bead of precum just for my pretty wife.

"You're lucky that I'm too fucking horny to punish your ass for this. I need to be inside this sweet, hot pussy." I run my finger under her thong and into her wet hole. "You're so damn ready for me." No hesitation. I move into position behind her and line up my cock with her entrance to slide into her warmth.

She grunts as I push deeper into her until my hips meet ass. "Fuck, Miles. You're too deep."

"No, I'm just where I belong and you're going to take this dick because you asked for it." I fist her hair, wrapping her ponytail through my fingers as I yank her head back. My tongue slides along her throat. "You are perfect, tempting, and all mine. You need to understand what you do to me. This dick is just a simple reminder. Do you understand?"

"Yes."

"I don't think you do." I pull back and then thrust forward, slamming hard. She gasps, gripping the pillows like her pussy is gripping my cock.

"Fuck me, show me that you're mine, Miles." Unable to stop, I take my other hand and pinch her taut nipples.

"I want to see your face as you come on my dick." I breakaway long enough to flip her onto her back and then slide back into her warmth, wrapping her legs around my waste. My mouth latches on to her sexy tits, one at a time, sucking and teasing each one, leaving my mark. She rolls her hips, grinding to find her orgasm, but it's my job to make her come and I better do it soon before I come. I reach between us and stroke her clit, rubbing her nub until she's gripping me and hollering my name.

"I love you, Miles."

"I love you too," I growl, pummeling her pussy until I unload every drop of cum I have left. We collapsed on the bed and she turns to see my new framed photo on the bedside table.

"Is that me?" It's the one of her that I took today. She's bent over working, and it came out like a damn masterpiece just like her.

"Of course, who else would that be?"

"But…" She picks it up and examines the photo even closer.

"Elsa, you look perfect doing what you love," I say, pulling her close for a kiss and take it from her to put it back where it belongs.

"You're nuts."

"For you."

EPILOGUE

MILES

SIX YEARS LATER

"Put your hands on my husband again, and there won't be enough luminol in the entire county to find a drop of your blood after I cut off every limb and dispose of your body," Elsa warns the drunken bride who had her wedding here last year—the same one I warned before.

"Oh my…" the woman says. She never made it to the first one, so I suppose this one panned out, but it's not looking good now.

"Don't 'oh my' me. I take someone touching my things very seriously," Elsa snaps, glaring daggers at the bold woman.

"You sound threatened." She laughs.

"And you sound stupid." I'm too stunned, and it's hard to think straight. Elsa's queen moves are turning me on so much that I might fuck her in the nearest damn room. I give her that warning look, and she just smirks because she knows what she did.

"Get out of here before you're thrown out." Damn, I love the way she takes control. The past several years we have lived an amazing life. Our first baby was born just last year and I can't wait to put another one inside her. The way she's behaving now, it's as if she's demanding I do it now.

"My husband owns half…"

"Erica, stop it right now. Let's go before I throw your ass in the trunk." He scolds his wife and then turns back to me. "I'm sorry, Miles." We shake hands and my wife steps to the side of me.

It's only then that he sees my stunningly beautiful wife and his tongue nearly falls from his mouth. He's lucky I'm civil. "Oh my God. This is the woman you told me about? You weren't kidding. She is the hottest woman in the world. No wonder my wife had to behave like a tramp."

"Why are you married to a whore like that?" Elsa blurts out.

"Because her daddy has what I want, and he wanted me to take her off his hands. A win-win, or so I thought." He rolls his eyes and then walks away.

"Mrs. Ivanov, a word?"

"Yes, I would like to speak with you in private, Mr. Ivanov," she huffs with the arrogance of someone who doesn't know her pussy is about to get pounded so hard she's about to have baby number two.

I hook my hand around her arm and gently guide my wife to the secure elevators that lead to my office, where I plan to violate her body until we're both completely satisfied and the territorial beast inside of her is sated.

My princess is just as obsessed with her dark prince.

ALSO BY C.M. STEELE

<u>A Best Friends Duet:</u>

Picture Perfect * Instant Obsession

<u>Best Friends Series:</u>

Always You * His Dirty Secret * Sleep Tight

<u>Bianchi Crime Family:</u>

Married to the Mob * Captured by the Mob * Owned by the Mob

<u>Cavanaugh Security Series:</u>

Protecting Macy * Securing Blake

<u>The Cline Brothers of Colorado:</u>

Whatever it Takes * Taking Whatever He Wants * Finding Paradise

<u>The Conti Crime Family Series:</u>

Alessio * Dario * Enrico * Matteo * Gio

<u>Dirty Boss Series:</u>

My Pet * My Cookie * My Flower * My Valentine

(Now on Audio)

<u>The Falling Hard & Fast Series:</u>

Falling for the Boss * Falling for the Enemy * Falling Hard

<u>The Fiore Family:</u>

Christmas with the Beast * Christmas with the Boss * Christmas with the Sheriff

<u>Gimme Series:</u>

Sugar * Luck * Rain * Cream * Heat * Love

Holly Hills Christmas:

Holiday's Cookies * Celeste's Secret * Bethany's Crush

(Now on Audio)

The James Family:

No Choice * No Way Out * No More Waiting

Keepsakes:

Keeping Blossom * Keep in Mind

The Lamian Wars:

Bound * Reveal * Release

All Hallows Eve

The Middleton Hotels:

Built for Me * Built to Last * Built Strong

Built Over Time * Built Overnight

Nothing but Trouble Series:

Taking the Bait * Taking the Mafia Princess

The O'Connell Family:

Claiming Red * Burning for Claire

Claiming Abby * Reminding Red

Obsessed Alpha Series:

Stone * Cole * Graham

Theo * Maddox * Alessandro

Tony * Cormack * Cameron * Jake * Sawyer

Reynolds Ranch Series:

Lara * Tobias

A Rocky Start Series:

Rocky Waters * Her Rock * Rocky Start

A Rough Hands Novella:

My Miracle * Nailing my Wife

Say Something Series:

Say Uncle * Say Please * Say Uncle: Doggy Style

Second Generation:

Say Yes

Seasons of Love:

Wet Summer * Autumn Falls * Winter Frost

Sister Switch:

Testing Her Professor * Assisting Her Boss

A Steele Christmas:

Mason's Winter * Perfectly Wrapped * The Company You Keep

A Steele Fairy Tale:

My Gold * My Forever * My Property * My Prince Charming

A Steele Riders Family Novella Series:

Sammie * Roxie * Mike * Dylan

Steele Riders MC Series:

Boomer * Mick * Jackson * Doc * Beast * Ghost

Wrench * Blade * Boss * Cowboy * Law *Cyber

Steele Riders MC 2ⁿᵈ Generation Series:

Will * Julian * Simon * Miles

Southern Hospitality:

Down South * Gone South

Sweet Temptation Bay:

A Taste Of Honey * The Mayor's Surrender * Trapped with my Stalker

Sweetheart's Treats:

Sweet Surprise * Doctor's Orders, Sweetheart * Sweet Surrender

Twin Sin:

Stalk Me Please * Sinful Intent

White Wolf Ridge Series:

Turner

Wolfe Creek Series:

Wolfe's Den * Beta: Her Alpha

Raging Kane * Written in History

Standalones:

Auctioned to the Kingpin* Buying Love * Christmas Compromise
* Conquering Alexandria

Ecstasy Captured * Grant's Deal * In Heat * Intense

Killer Abs * Love Discovered * Loving My Neighbor *
Lucky Ride

Mrs. Valentine * My Christmas Gift

Rainy Days * Stormy Nights * Red Hot Nights

Room Service * Scarred * Sharp Curves

So Wrong * Standing There

The Mobster's Virgin * The Wedding Guest * Unexpected